Shadow Cat Summer

Rebecca Smith

Illustrated by Dawn Treacher

Stairwell Books //

Published by Stairwell Books
161 Lowther Street
York, YO31 7LZ

www.stairwellbooks.co.uk
@stairwellbooks

ISBN: 978-1-913432-26-3

Layout design: Alan Gillott
Cover art and illustrations: Dawn Treacher
P10

For Harry, Daisy and Eddie
with all my love.

Chapter 1

London

You might think it's lovely living on a houseboat. Sometimes you would be right. It's lovely when it's sunny and you get up early and see birds and other boats going by, and eat your breakfast outside, or stay up late and look at the stars and the lights dancing on the black water. We have a string of coloured lightbulbs and paper lanterns for parties. But a lot of the time you'd be wrong. Sometimes it is freezing and smelly and our clothes are never dry. The wind is salty even though we're miles from the sea, and suddenly our lips crack and we get cracks on our fingers, like the world's deepest ever papercuts. Maybe an evil papercut demon sails down the Thames and sneaks on board in the night. Even now in summer it can be really cold.

On our boat everything is tiny and everything really should be kept tidy. When your only space in the world is this small, you can't leave a mess, or keep stuff you don't need. One time our mum even made us chuck away things out of party bags on the way home from a party.

All the rooms go into each other. That's annoying. Mum has a bedroom to herself up at the bow, but she practices her viola wherever she likes, often on deck when it's not too cold. Alex and I have to share a bedroom, which is not good when you are eleven. Mum put a curtain up to try to make separate spaces, but it doesn't really work. We always know what the other one is doing, even what they're thinking...

Katrina McCloud looked up from her work. She realised she was doing what Mr. Morgan called "digressing". They were meant to be writing about "Where I Live". She glanced across the classroom to see what Alex was doing, even though she knew he'd be at the illustrating stage already. He never wrote much, just wanted to draw and draw and draw. Katrina wondered what exactly she should draw. A picture of their houseboat that morning wouldn't have been very nice. Her mum had been banging about in the bedroom, playing horrible, scratchy music, and not bothering to see if they had breakfast (they did, cornflakes with no milk) or even if they went to school.

Katrina wondered if she would ever write the truth about what life on The Bluebell was like. Somehow, she and Alex had always known that they weren't meant to talk about some things. It was as though they had a secret, a dark, shadowy thing that lurked, and sometimes went away, but then suddenly came back and yowled, and nobody talked about it being there.

She crossed out the bit about the party bags, not with one neat ruled line, the way they were meant to, but with black, angry scratches of pen that almost ripped through the paper.

She got up and went over to look at how Alex was getting on. He was drawing a picture of The Bluebell, a cross-section, so that you could see how all the rooms connected and what was inside them. She knew that he would go on to add a view under the water with freshwater fish and plants and little creatures that only he knew the names of. His pictures always looked perfect. Funny that you could be twins but not good at the same stuff. She wished she'd got some of the drawing skills. And Alex could have done with a bit more of the boldness that she had. Though it was only people he was timid with, the sort of people who laughed when they found out that his real name was Alexei, and who asked rude questions about their dad, and how come they couldn't speak Russian.

Chapter 2

Scotland – North of Inverness – The same day

The farmer and the vet looked at where the sheep's windpipe had been. Much of the body was gone too. What remained was damp and stained red and brown. Flies buzzed around it. Decay was setting in already. The other sheep cropped the grass, occasionally baa-ing to each other, keeping clear of the men and the horrible find.

'Well, none of us likes to see it. She was a fine ewe,' the farmer said, rubbing his handkerchief across his brow.

'You've told the police already?'

'Aye, and not just for the insurance. If there's some rogue dog about, we have to put a stop to it.'

'This doesn't look typical of a rogue dog,' said the vet.

'My two woke us. You know them, Ed, they're good girls,' said the farmer. 'Going crazy. Thought we had a burglar. But when I

4

went to see if there was someone in the yard, they just whimpered and refused to come. I've never seen them like that before. They're working dogs! Behaving like a couple of rabbits, they were. My wife said she heard this yowling, something like a fox, but not. Must have been the rogue dog folk have been talking about. Shone the torch around the yard, but I couldnae see anything. I came up here this morning, all the sheep were huddled up in the far corner, and then this…'

'I hope she'll be the only one you lose.'

'Aye. Three it was in the winter. And Murdo McPherson lost two last month. It's got to be stopped.' He stomped off towards the Land Rover.

Ed Stirling was still thought of as "The New Vet" even though he'd joined the practice five years ago. He'd grown up in Edinburgh and worked all over the world, but he loved this place. It was where his grandmother was from. He knelt in the rough grass and looked at the deep red trenches on the sheep's back.

The farmer returned with some old sacks and threw them over the remains.

'Keep the crows off until the police get here.'

In silence, the two men looked about for large stones to weigh the sacks down.

Ed drove off. He had a few more calls to make that morning, and surgery to run that afternoon too. He saw the green and yellow Land Rover that belonged to his friend, Archie Carmichael, coming towards him, so he pulled into a passing place and flashed his lights. Archie stopped and rolled down the window.

5

'Nasty kill up there,' Ed said, indicating the field behind him. 'Jim McIntyre's lost a ewe.'

'Shame. Whose dog was it?' Archie asked. 'Tourist, I suppose. July, eh? Did he see anything?'

'Thought he heard something in the night. Sheep was in a terrible state. He's called the police.'

'I'll keep an eye out,' said Archie. With a brief nod he pulled away.

Archie Carmichael spent his day much as he always did; a few phone calls and emails at the Visitor Centre, and then he was out in the forest. That day he had to repaint some of the markers on one of the trails, and he'd decided to divert another path away from where he knew there was a pine marten family. More time at the Visitor Centre in the afternoon, and then he was home for his tea.

The Carmichael's cottage was half a mile up its own little track. His wife, Clara, had made one of the outbuildings into a studio. He could see her framed in the window, bent over her work. She was a wildlife artist; a successful one too. There were t. shirts and birthday cards, tea towels and calendars of her watercolours of birds, otters, pine martens, red squirrels and wild cats. The wild cat pictures had to be done from photos of captive ones and from the imagination. Clara knew as well as Archie, that almost anybody who thinks they spot a Scottish wild cat is mistaken.

Archie parked beside the crumbling barn that they were going to make into a holiday cottage, crunched across the gravel, and knocked on the studio door. He waited for her to say "come in". He would never have gone in uninvited. He expected her to be happy after a whole day of peace, a whole day to paint, but she looked worried. Nothing in the studio looked quite right. The flowers in the jam jar on the windowsill were wilting, and the picture of puffins she'd been working on looked hardly different from that morning. There was an uneaten sandwich on the table (her lunch? not eaten at almost five?) and her phone was in there too. Clara never took her phone into her studio.

'What's wrong?' he asked.

'I'm worried about Chrissie. She won't answer her phone. I've left endless messages, but she's ignoring them. It's always switched off. And I'm even more worried about Katrina and Alex.'

Chapter 3

London

Katrina and Alex always walked home from school by themselves. That day, at four o'clock, the tide was on the way out, but there was just enough water for the pontoons to bob and sway. They loved it that the tides made such a difference here, in the middle of London, so far from the sea. But as soon as they saw The Bluebell, they knew that something was very wrong.

'Uh?' said Alex.

'Oh no!' said Katrina.

The door to the cabin was wide open. There was a lot of stuff pegged out, but it wasn't clean washing. It was their mother's concert clothes at crazy angles. A black silk dress was hanging sideways from its skirt, a green velvet shawl hung by one peg and was trailing on the floor like a defeated flag, a purple dress had

8

been flung across a bench, and lay there, as though it had been assassinated. There were sheets of music, damp and torn, pinned up among the clothes. Her aquamarine dress, the one they really loved, was dripping wet and muddy, like something dragged out of the river. Her two good jackets, her pretty scarves and skirts and tops were all hanging there or crumpled in heaps on the deck.

And Mum always complained about how you couldn't wash most of this stuff. They were always being sent to collect things from the dry cleaners when she was getting ready for a concert and was late as usual.

'Maybe she accidentally dropped it overboard and decided to wash it instead, or just dry it out or something...' said Alex. Katrina just looked at him. They both really knew what must have been happening.

And when they got closer it was even worse. There was blood, mostly dried and brown, splattered on the deck and smeared on the clothes and on the sheets of music. And there was silence.

'Mum,' called Katrina, clutching at her brother's arm. 'Mum, are you there?'

No answer.

They went into the cabin.

'Oh no!' said Alex. The mirror had been smashed. The gold frame with its carved roses and leaves was still in one piece, but there were lethal jags of glass everywhere, all over the floor, and in the otherwise empty viola case. Alex gently closed it and ran his finger across the worn silver lettering – *Chrissie McCloud* – then he opened it again and left it as it had been. He'd felt as though he were closing a coffin.

'We have to mind where we walk,' said Katrina. And then Mr. Tom came running in, meowing.

'His paws!' shouted Alex. Katrina lunged and scooped Mr. Tom up.

'We'll shut him in our room,' she said. 'It might be alright in there.' She picked him up and buried her face in the soft ginger fur. She would have liked to cry into it, to curl up on the bed with him and sob and sob. But she didn't, they had to be tougher than that. They had to sort things out.

They crunched across the splinters of glass, through the kitchen and into their bedroom. There was a trail of their mother's clothes, but nothing broken. They put Mr. Tom down on Alex's bed. It was the one that they both knew he preferred because it got more sun, although normally Katrina would have denied it and kept trying to settle him on hers.

'I wonder if he's had any food,' she said.

'I gave him some biscuits this morning,' said Alex, 'all that was left in the box. He'd run out of the smelly stuff.'

'Maybe she got him some more.'

'Maybe.' They shut Mr. Tom in the bedroom and picked their way back to the kitchen.

'It's lucky we're both wearing trainers,' said Katrina. Yesterday she had been moaning that she was the only girl in the class who didn't have any summer shoes and it was nearly the end of term. She bit her lip. Perhaps, she thought, if she hadn't complained her mum wouldn't have been so upset. Now they didn't even know where she was. Katrina felt the familiar muddy sludge of guilt and worry settle inside her. Their mum's phone was on the windowsill behind the sink where she always left it. The battery was dead. Alex plugged it in to charge.

The twins had washed up and put away their bowls from breakfast, not that dry cornflakes made much of a mess. Now there were three mugs of black coffee, half-empty, in the sink, and a vodka bottle, completely empty, on the draining board.

'I thought she had been drinking yesterday,' said Alex. 'She had that horrible smell.'

'Me too. We should have said something.'

'I never know how.'

'Me neither.'

'Do you think we should go and look for her? She might be hurt somewhere,' said Alex.

'Or somebody horrible might get hold of her,' said Katrina. 'What if she fell overboard, or off the pontoon?' They looked out of the kitchen's tiny porthole, as though they might spot her through that. There was now just a thin layer of water over the mud. Could she be lying face down in it somewhere?

'We didn't check her bedroom, or the bathroom,' said Alex. 'Come on!' Bubbles of hope and fear rose up inside them, though they both knew that she wasn't on the boat at all. They had sensed her absence immediately. They found a boulder of towels and more of their mum's clothes in the bathroom. All her lotions and potions had been knocked into the bath. Lots were spilled, but none were broken. It looked as though it had been an accident, a clumsy stumbling or grasping-at-something accident. Her bedroom was worse, but she wasn't there either.

'She's always come back eventually before,' said Katrina.

A picture of her mum being brought back by a sinister taxi driver who'd wanted to come onto the boat, who'd leered at her and said, "Not got a man here to look after you, then?" flashed into her mind.

'Maybe she's with a friend,' said Alex.

'Yeah, like who?' said Katrina.

'Someone from the orchestra or something?' Alex tried to sound hopeful.

'But they've all gone, haven't they? They're all on tour except her. It started today. It's on the calendar. I'm sure that's why she's gone so ...you know…'

'Maybe she had to stay to look after us. But Aunty Clara could have come here like last year…'

'I've got a feeling they didn't ask Mum. They didn't want her. She was so cross after the last rehearsal. Maybe they cancelled her place on the tour.' The twins looked around the kitchen. Everything was horrible.

'Well there's no cat food and nothing for tea. We'll have to go and get something for Mr. Tom anyway. And we can look for her at the same time. I've got £20 in my pig,' said Katrina.

'I've got £12 something too.'

When they went back into their bedroom Mr. Tom made a dash for the door, but Alex caught him.

'You have to stay in here till we've cleared up. Sorry,' he said, putting him back on the bed.

Katrina took the stopper out of her pig. The four five pound notes were gone. There was nothing but a scrap of paper inside, and on it scrawled

I owe you £20
Signed Mum.

They stared at it, neither of them wanting to say anything.

'Here's my money anyway,' said Alex. He untied the knot in the end of a football sock and tipped it onto his bed. £12.43.

'At least we can get some cat food,' said Katrina.

'And maybe some chips,' said Alex.

The streets were hot and crowded with people leaving work early because it was a Friday and summer. The cafés and bars were packed, the pavement tables were full, and the braying laughter of grown-ups was spilling outwards, so thick that moving through it seemed difficult. Their mum probably wouldn't have been in one of those posh, noisy places, but they looked anyway. She could be anywhere. They were remembering the last time, a rainy Sunday night in February, when they had found her crying in the doorway of a florist after she hadn't come home after a rehearsal.

Soon they were at Mini-Market, the shop they went to most often. There weren't many proper shops near where they lived. It was all estate agents, and perfume shops and clothes shops where things were so expensive that there were no prices in the windows. The only shop Alex liked was the one selling artists' materials. He had been planning to buy some proper watercolours and more brushes. Aunty Clara had given him some at Christmas, but now the paints were nearly all gone.

Mum wasn't in Mini-Market. Alex carried the basket and they chose Go-Cat biscuits and Felix in Gravy for Mr. Tom. There wasn't much choice.

'He'll lick off the gravy and leave the rest,' said Alex.

'Well Kit-e-Kat always makes him throw up,' said Katrina. 'If we get a big thing of milk we can have cereal for dinner and breakfast. There were quite a lot of cornflakes.'

The queue at the checkout was long.

'Some chips would be nice,' said Alex. 'And we could carry on looking for Mum as we went.'

'Ok. But we should try to save some of the money. No fish for Mr. Tom.'

Katrina thought that she would feel funny eating chips, guilty really, when their mum was lost. Would Mum be cross if she came back whilst they were eating them and think that they hadn't been bothered about her being gone and were really greedy? And what if she didn't come back that night? Or tomorrow?

Mini-Market was run by two middle-aged brothers. The one the twins called The Nasty One was behind the till. He always looked at them as though they were about to steal something. If it had been The Nice One they might have asked him if he'd seen her.

The Nasty One pushed their change across the counter towards them.

'Your mum was in here this morning,' he said. 'She very bad, very, very bad.' He made a horrible gesture of drinking. 'She needs to see the doctor. You take her to doctor. You got a dad? Make sure he take her.'

14

'We will,' said Katrina. She took the change and pushed Alex ahead of her, out of the shop.

'We should have asked what time he saw her,' said Alex, once they were outside.

'He said "this morning". And he's horrible. I don't want to ask him for help.' Katrina knew that Alex was sharing her thought: If only we *did* have a dad to take her to the doctor.

They walked the few streets further to the chip shop and then hurried home. Nothing had changed on the deck of the boat. She definitely hadn't come back. They sat on the pontoon and ate the chips, dangling their legs over the mud, not wanting to be back among the spoilt clothes and blood and broken glass. When they had almost finished and were thinking about throwing the last few scraps to a swan and her three cygnets, they heard their mum's phone ringing.

Maybe it was her. They sprinted, leapt on board, crunched and slipped across the broken glass and into the kitchen. Alex grabbed the phone and said hello. A soft, familiar voice said, 'Alex, is that you?'

Aunty Clara.

Alex couldn't make his voice work. The out-of-breathness from running and chips turned into sniffing and gulping.

'Don't!' Katrina hissed at him, but it was too late, Aunty Clara had heard. Alex let his sister take the phone.

'He's a bit upset,' Katrina said.

'Is Alex hurt? Where's your mum? Is she at a concert?'

'We're alright,' said Katrina. 'We just haven't had a very good day.'

'But where's your mum?'

'Um…we're not sure,' said Katrina.

'She hasn't gone on tour and left you alone, has she? You shouldn't be on your own on a boat in the middle of London. She was meant to be telling me what was happening. Is she alright?'

'Um,' said Katrina.

'Come on, I'm her sister and your aunty. What's going on down there? I know there's something. I had that feeling. Tell me, or I'll just have to get the first plane down and find out.'

'Really? Would you really?' said Katrina, realising at once that she'd given it away, and Mum might be cross if they didn't keep things private.

'Tell me what's wrong,' said Aunty Clara. Then it was Katrina's turn to start sniffing and gulping.

Chapter 4

It was a scratchy, painful, unearthly sound; not like music at all. There were cuts on the musician's arms and hands, her dress was torn, her hair tangled, her face swollen from tears and vodka. People were keeping their distance from her. Even in the evening rush-hour nobody came close enough to smell the river on her clothes, or the sadness and alcohol on her breath. And nobody put any money on the black velvet scarf she had spread on the floor in front of her. She knew that the music wasn't right, and knowing this made her cry as she played.

Wave after wave of passengers hurried by, averting their eyes, trying not to hear the broken melody. The evening turned to night, the gaps between the trains grew longer, and the musician lay on the cold ground. Metal shutters tumbled down, and the station was left to the rats.

Chapter 5

Scotland

Archie hated it when Clara went away. They normally had a harmonious life together. Whilst he was at the Visitor Centre, or in the forest or on the mountains, trying to keep the people safe from nature and his beloved bit of the Highlands safe from the people, Clara would usually be at work in her studio, or teaching art classes for adults at the local college. He liked it best when she spent the day near him, bringing her paints, working close to wherever he was. He hated it when she went away. And he missed his dog. He'd had Bobbie since he was a teenager. It was four months since he'd died, and he still missed him all the time. You needed a dog up here. He had been a really fine dog, a collie-cross. The rug in front of the fireplace still looked empty.

Archie sat in his chair and looked across to where Clara should be sitting. Their faded old sofa had a dent where she would normally be reading or sometimes sewing, but most often sketching. Clara drew nearly all the time; even if she were watching TV she'd be drawing what was happening, or him watching it. He was so used to it now that it didn't make him self-conscious. Archie poured his daily shot of the malt whisky that was made just a few miles away. He could smell the bracken and peat in it.

Sometimes he hated Clara's sister. She was bloody irresponsible, disappearing off, leaving his nephew and niece by themselves in the middle of the city. Drinking too much.

He looked out of the window. The violet dusk was falling across the valley. Yesterday's left-over lasagne was waiting for him in the fridge. Please, he thought, let her be back soon. And then the phone began to ring. He was across the room in two bounds. Little ridges of dried mud fell from the boots, that without Clara there to remind him, he hadn't bothered to take off.

'Archie, it's me. They've found her.' Clara's voice seemed to have more of London in it after just one day.

'Ach, thank God! Is she alright?'

'She was in a really bad way. She was found this morning. She was in a tube station. She'd probably collapsed and spent the night there, so at least she wasn't on the street somewhere...'

'And the children?'

'They're being very brave. We've been to see Chrissie. She's in hospital. She looked terrible, just crying, her arms all cut from a broken mirror. At least they'd given her a bath.'

'So, what now? Can you come home? Bring the children and come home?'

19

'I'm going to try to get flights tomorrow or the next day. The twins can stay for the whole summer. The hospital said they'll keep Chrissie in, try to stabilise her, dry her out, find her a place in a clinic if she's lucky.'

'Aye, good.'

'And Archie, don't forget to shut the hens up, will you?'

'The hens? Oh no, I'll not forget them!'

The hens! He had forgotten them. It was almost completely dark now. He emptied his glass and went to shut them up, taking the torch so that he could check they were all in. Clara loved those hens. She had four black and white Speckledies, three Black Rocks, and a Rhode Island Red with a funny foot. People say hens are silly birds, but they are very sensible when it comes to bedtime. They always go home to roost, but you have to be sure they are safely locked away at night.

The moon was up, but it wasn't full, and there were some clouds. Archie heard the shivery hoot of a tawny owl, and he smiled as he walked down the path towards the henhouse. Then he froze. There was something there. The shadows were different. Something made the hairs on the back of his neck stand up. There was a darkness in the shadows, and he knew that something was watching him. What was it? Had he come out just in time? He hardly dared to move his arm – this was ridiculous – here he was six foot two and thirty-three years old – a forest ranger – spooked by a fox – scared to shine a torch in his own back garden. He forced himself to do it. He swung an arc of yellow light across the path and over the henhouse. Nothing. But he could feel it there, the thing, the presence, watching him. He shone the torch towards the brambles at the bottom of the garden where his little patch of civilisation melted into the woods. Nothing. He took a few steps closer to the henhouse, he was almost there now. He carried on waving the torch, making stripes of brightness. Archie shut the hens' little door and locked it. He started to slowly back his way towards the house. He mustn't turn his back on the thing, he sensed that. He knew that. He carried on sending arcs of light around the henhouse, across the garden, into the woods. Nothing. He was almost back at the house when the beam caught something – two silver discs shone back at him. He froze – remembered his ranger's whistle – it was there around his neck – he blew and blew – shrieking and shrill.

The discs were gone. They had only been there for a moment, if they'd been there at all. He stumbled back into the house and locked the door. He hurried from room to room, closing windows, making sure they were properly shut, then he checked the front door and the back door again.

He collapsed on the sofa and laughed and laughed. He poured himself another wee shot and laughed some more. Thank God nobody could see him, that there was nobody for miles, probably nobody would have heard that whistle. They'd call him a Big Jessie – scared of a fox! His nephew and niece in London would've been braver than he was.

Chapter 6

London

This is what they packed:

Alex
grey hoodie
green hoodie
blue hoodie (Highland summers can be like London winters)
2 pairs of cut-offs
1 pair of jeans
4 t-shirts
pants and socks
box of pencils and sharpener and rubber
drawing book
sock with what was left of the money
Cosmic by Frank Cottrell Boyce

Boris (the bear their dad had sent on their second birthday)

Animal Tracker Kit (birthday present from Uncle Archie and Aunty Clara – he hadn't had a chance to use it yet).

Katrina

exactly same clothes as Alex, but one hoodie was a sort of raspberry colour, instead of grey

flute and music folder

notebook and pencil case (a black and white cat whose tummy unzipped)

When Hitler Stole Pink Rabbit by Judith Kerr which she had just started

Igor the Tiger (a toy Siberian tiger their dad had sent on their second birthday. Also known as Igger the Tigger.)

Swiss army knife (the Explorer model). Alex's had fallen over the side of the boat but when they looked at low tide, hoping it would be there in the mud, it was gone. It normally lived in her pocket, but Aunty Clara said she wouldn't be allowed to take it on the plane without being mistaken for a terrorist. It had to go in the hold.

Mr. Tom

old wicker cat carrier (if you can say that someone is taking something they are travelling inside)

fleece blanket from Alex's bed (inside the cat carrier)

two catnip mice (also inside the cat carrier – smell faded)

bottle of water, dish, Go-Cat crunchies for the journey.

'I've always wished he was the sort of cat who went on a collar and lead,' said Katrina, poking her fingers through the wicker and trying to calm Mr. Tom who was meowing pitifully. 'He thinks he's going to the V E T.'

Mr. Tom had never been on a plane before; they'd always left him behind, with one of the other boat people to feed him, but Aunty Clara said that he'd better come. They might be away for the whole summer, and anyway, he would miss them too much.

They tidied up the boat as best they could and put all the plants on deck in a big tub of water.

'It feels wrong,' said Alex, 'leaving The Bluebell and leaving Mum.'

'She's in the best place,' said Clara. 'She can only get better in a clinic.' But Mr. Tom carried on meowing and Katrina and Alex just looked glum. Then Brian and Pippa from The Good Tern, two boats down came along. They looked exactly like the sort of people you'd imagine living on a houseboat. Brian had a white beard and Pippa wore a beret and boaty sorts of clothes, stripy tops and rolled-up navy-blue trousers. She even had a skirt with pictures of yachts on it.

'Off somewhere?' Pippa called, seeing the rucksacks and the cat carrier.

'Scotland with me for the summer,' Aunty Clara called back.

'Oh, I thought you were Chrissie! You look so alike.'

Everybody said that. They had the same tangled curls and dark sapphire eyes, but Clara was much softer-looking. Chrissie had a sharper nose and was much skinnier. People would have guessed that Clara was the twin's mum and Chrissie their artist aunty, not the other way round.

'I'm their aunty. Their mum's in hospital. She's very depressed, in a bit of a bad way.'

'I'm so sorry,' said Pippa. 'I hadn't noticed anything wrong.'

'She went downhill very fast,' said Chrissie.

'Twins,' said Pippa. 'You can always come to us if you need help.'

Alex and Katrina looked at their feet, not wanting to say anything, not wanting to admit their mother's failings until -

'Thanks,' Katrina managed to mumble.

'Here,' said Brian, 'some spending money for the holidays.' He took out one of the red spotty handkerchiefs he always used – either as a bandana like a pirate or to hold screws and bits when he was fixing things – they had never seen him blow his nose on one. He put something inside it and tossed it across the pontoon to them. Katrina caught it deftly.

When they opened it later (it seemed rude to open it whilst Pippa and Brian were nearby) they found two twenty-pound notes and seven pound coins.

'It's very nice of him,' said Clara, 'and I'm pleased the hanky was clean, but you know there isn't much to buy where we are. You have to walk miles just to buy an ice cream…'

Scotland

Velvet in darkness, she moves through the night, a silent shadow, claws sheathed. She pads across the needles, pine-sharp, knowing everything. Here there were people. Here they sat, scuffed their heavy feet. Wood pigeons roost above

her. She smells the warmth of feathers, the soft pink-grey flesh of them. An owl calls – sister owl – fellow hunter. She feels the wind of her wings.

She stops, waits, listens, knows, moves on, follows the stream. All creatures must drink, deer must drink. Deer may be here.

Softly, softly, the water falls, down, down between the trees. She meets the moonlight at the loch. Here are rocks, big enough to hide beneath. Here she drinks. Here, sometimes, she brings her feast. At dawn she will hunt, but here, tonight, she sleeps.

Chapter 7

Scotland

Uncle Archie was waiting at the airport to meet them. They spotted him before he saw them coming through Arrivals. Katrina thought that there seemed something sad about him standing there in his green work clothes. Then she realised it was because he was all alone. He'd always brought Bobbie to meet them, and there had been licks and jumpings up and "Get Down Boy!"'s with the big hugs. But when he did spot them he grinned and threw his arms wide, and the big hugs were still there. Katrina couldn't help being a bit relieved that Mr. Tom wouldn't have a dog to contend with.

'We're really sorry about Bobbie,' she said.

'He was a good age for a dog,' said Uncle Archie. 'And I'm really sorry your mum's in a bad way.'

They passed the shop selling magazines and chocolate and Scottish souvenirs for people who had forgotten to buy a present for somebody.

'It's amazing how far away you can get in a day if you try,' Alex said as they climbed into their uncle's Land Rover. It was better than Aunty Clara's old Renault. Their mum didn't have a car. She said there was no point having one in London, though they knew it was also because they couldn't afford it. 'If we were at school, we'd only just be going out to lunchtime play.'

'1047 kilometres,' said Katrina, who was looking at the mileage calculator in Archie's *AA Road Atlas of Great Britain*. She pictured the TV weather map. Now they were right up near the top. 1047 kilometres away from Mum and The Bluebell and normal life.

They were soon away from the airport, and through the city. Mr. Tom, who'd managed to sleep for the last few hours woke up and began to meow.

'Don't worry, we'll soon be there,' Alex whispered through the wicker of the basket.

'We'll have to keep him shut in,' said Aunty Clara.

'Aye,' said Archie. 'We don't want him setting out for London, do we?'

Mr Tom kept meowing for the thirty-five minutes it took them to get to the Carmichael's cottage. Katrina noticed that the big wooden gate to the driveway wasn't closed. She usually loved jumping out of the car and holding it open whilst the others drove through, leaning back against the hedge to be certain there was room, then putting the heavy iron bolt down to keep it closed, and climbing back into the car for the little ride up to the house. She supposed that Uncle Archie didn't bother with it now that Bobbie wasn't there, or perhaps he'd just left it open because they were coming straight back. She and Alex usually liked running down to the gate when they had nothing much to do (which was a lot of the time when they were in Scotland) and just sitting on it to look out over the glen. They could see forest and one end of the loch and to the mountains beyond. Today, though, she slumped down in her seat and let herself be carried up to the house. Being here without Mum seemed all wrong. It wasn't a summer holiday – it was a fake summer holiday, a pretend one.

Once they'd settled Mr. Tom in a spare bedroom with a litter tray and some food and his blanket on the bed, they went to unpack their own things. They loved the rooms that Aunty Clara called theirs, even though other visitors sometimes got to stay in them. Your own room in an attic is a treat when you're used to just a small slice of a boat. The stairs were extra creaky, and at the top was a tiny landing, only big enough for one person at a time. Here were two doors with old-fashioned latches that you lifted. A room each.

There were patchwork quilts that Aunty Clara had made in greens and greys and heathers – moorland colours. Just looking at them made the twins want to fling themselves down and sleep forever. Could you get jetlag without crossing a time-zone? It felt like jetlag, but maybe it was something else. Katrina unpacked and put Igor the Tiger on her pillow. Alex decided he couldn't be bothered to do anything and left his stuff in his rucksack.

Each room had a desk under the window, a little bookcase, with one empty shelf for the visitor's books (the others were filled with interesting ones that you would normally want to read), and a chest of drawers. There were only a few places where you could stand up in each room because the ceilings were so slopey. There wasn't room for much else, and certainly not a wardrobe, but the twins didn't wear the sort of clothes that had to be hung up. The miniature windows looked out over the roof of Clara's studio. You could see the henhouse, the old barn, the tree where there was an *almost* dangerously frayed hammock and a tyre on a rope that wasn't dangerously frayed, and then beyond the garden to the forest. Alex thought back to last summer, to his mum falling asleep in that hammock, a big empty wine glass on the grass beneath her. He blinked the memory away and tried to think about something else. There were pictures of birds and plants and animals by Aunty Clara and other artists that she liked, as well as some that he and Katrina had done on previous visits. Alex looked critically at them. He remembered drawing that otter during the autumn half-term last year and knowing that there was something wrong with it that he couldn't see. Now he saw that the legs were too stubby. He flung himself down on the bed and wished he was back on The Bluebell, and that everything was normal. He could see across the landing into Katrina's room. She was collapsed on her bed too, her face buried in the pillow, but he could tell that she wasn't asleep.

The next morning, picking at one of the huge breakfasts that they were always given in Scotland, Alex said, 'Aunty Clara, if you do a picture and you know there's something wrong with it, but you can't see what it is, wouldn't you want people to tell you before it is finished?'

'Of course I would,' said Clara. 'Or, I think I would. Some artists hate people saying anything about what they're working on. I guess it depends how people say it.'

'Well, I hate it when people just say "Oh, it's lovely" about my pictures because I'm only eleven, and they are just thinking "Oh, that's good for eleven." That otter I did last year, the one that's up in my room, its legs are too stubby. I hate looking at it now. I think people should tell the truth and not say things are great when there's really something wrong.'

'That's a very mature attitude,' Uncle Archie said, coming in ready for work in his green trousers and green jumper with the elbow patches.

'Mum thinks you should always say that everything's lovely,' said Katrina, who had been too busy scraping out the last bits of her egg to say anything before. 'It's awful. She always wants to pretend that everything is just perfect. She'd get really cross if someone said something about her playing. I think she had a big row with the orchestra, and then they went on tour without her. But she wouldn't say. She'll never say about anything.' Katrina absentmindedly turned the empty eggshell upside-down in the egg cup. Was it possible to eat a soft-boiled egg without doing that? Even if she were grown-up and all alone she would do it. 'But your hens' eggs, Aunty Clara, they really are lovely. Always lovely.'

The yolks were so yellow and tasty, exactly the same shade as Cadmium Yellow in Alex's watercolours. 'I like it,' Katrina went on, 'when Mrs. Heald tells me in my flute lesson how I can do something better.'

'Well, not all artists are as mature as you,' said Uncle Archie, kissing her on the top of her head as he went to put his boots on. 'You'll all come and meet me for lunch at the Centre? What do you think, Alex?'

Alex was gazing out of the window. He hadn't been listening.

'Alex, are you ok?'

Alex pulled a face.

'I just wonder how Mum is,' he said.

'She'll be ok,' said Aunty Clara. 'She's in the best place.'

The best place? thought Alex. That was like what people said when somebody had died. She's Gone To A Better Place.

After breakfast Mr. Tom seemed so calm that they decided to let him wander about the rest of the house. They checked that all the windows and doors were shut and then let him explore. He went from room to room sniffing everywhere.

'He can probably smell Bobbie. He's probably concerned that there's a dog about. He'll be ok when he realises that he has the place to himself,' said Clara.

'Barge cats have to be adaptable,' said Katrina.

'And brave,' said Alex. 'They never know when there might be a seagull about to dive-bomb their home or a vicious dog running along the bank. And people think they have a right to stroke them, just like they think they have a right to stare through your windows.' In the end Mr. Tom settled down next to the fire.

'He'll have to wait a couple months before we light it again. We don't normally need it in July and August, usually in September though...' said Clara.

As if he had heard her, Mr. Tom got up and moved to a windowsill where the sun through the glass had warmed the old wood. The windowsills were so deep that you could sit on them and close the curtains to hide yourself. If you kept still and quiet, nobody would know you were there. Mr. Tom sat and looked out at the garden.

'Now he's watching the hens,' said Katrina. 'Are cats and hens alright together?'

'Always,' said Aunty Clara. 'Just think, a few thousand years of farmyards with cats and hens together. They know to leave each other alone. Maybe the cats don't think of the hens as being birds. A kitten only has to run at a hen a couple of times to find out how fierce a chicken can be – all that flapping and noise and big claws and a beak. No, cats and hens usually like each other's company. Cats will sit and watch the hens, quite companionable.'

Alex went over and buried his face in Mr. Tom's dense fur. He stayed like that for a long time. When he looked up his eyes were red.

'Can we ring up that clinic and see how Mum is. When might she be better?'

'It's going to take a while. It wouldn't be good for her to come out until she's really sorted, mentally and physically. But let's ring up now anyway.'

Aunty Clara dialed the number and then stood there, looking out of the window with Mr. Tom. It seemed to be a clinic that didn't pick up the phone.

'Maybe they have phoneaphobics too,' said Katrina, forcing a smile. But she pictured her Mum locked up, like a burglar in a cartoon.

At last somebody answered, but they said that Chrissie was "In A Session" and couldn't be disturbed, and that they should try between 5pm and 6pm that evening, that "contact with family and friends often wasn't helpful at this stage".

'Go and play outside, twins,' said Aunty Clara. 'It might cheer you up. But put some of this bug stuff on first. Remember, you have to put it on every day up here. Extra when we're going out with Archie in the forest.'

'Yeah, yeah,' said Katrina. 'We couldn't forget about Highland midges, could we?' They slathered themselves in the goo. It had a lemony scent, which wasn't really that bad, as long as you didn't accidentally lick your hand. They went outside, and took turns on the tyre swing, and watched the chickens. When they got bored, they used Katrina's knife to carve their initials and the outlines of two tiny clouds into a tree in a place where they thought nobody would ever see.

They wandered over to the old barn. Katrina pushed gently on the huge wooden door and it swung open. The sun streamed in through the few windows and motes of ancient dust danced in the golden rays. There was nothing much inside; only some ancient bales of straw, an old cart that looked like something a donkey could pull, some broken deckchairs with faded green seats, and some wooden boxes with strange rusty tools inside. The twins stared at them. They were like ones they'd seen on a school trip to the most boring museum in the world. They'd

34

called it The Museum of Stupid Things, and now they couldn't remember what its real name had been.

They climbed the wooden ladder to the second storey. Aunty Clara called it the hay loft, but it seemed more like a giant shelf. It covered about half the area of the barn. The twins used to find it exciting because there was no railing; you could easily fall down, and if you did you would probably die. They'd wished that there were great heaps of hay that they could leap into. There were still lots of bales of old straw in the loft, and they flopped down onto them. In the past they'd played spying games – lurking in the loft to watch whatever (usually nothing) was going on down below, hoping that somebody would come into the barn and not know they were there. There were skylight windows, very dusty and cobwebby. The twins lay on their backs and watched the clouds passing over them.

'I wish this was my house,' said Katrina.

'I don't,' said Alex. 'I just want to go home.' Pictures of Mum in the clinic, her arms cut, her hair bedraggled, her face puffy and yellow, and then that horrible smell seemed to drift across the skylight with the clouds. 'Well, kind of,' he added. 'I don't know where I want to be.' He got up from the bales – the straw was itchy and digging through his t-shirt anyway – and walked over to one of the little side windows. He knelt down to look out over the countryside. There were flies and moths caught in the cobwebs and lying dead on the sill. You could see for miles, but they were surrounded, hemmed in by mountains and forest. 'But we're here,' he said, 'a thousand miles from nowhere.' Alex pressed one hand against the window and left a print in the ancient dust.

Chapter 8

The holidays had already started in Scotland, so there were no school parties, just the usual straggles of walkers, and Archie wasn't that busy when they arrived for lunch. They sat on the log benches outside the Centre. Each one had been carved from a huge fallen tree. They were surprisingly comfortable.

Clara and Archie made good picnics, but it helped that things that seemed boring in London were quite tasty in Scotland. Oatcakes with cheese or glued together with heather honey were their favourites. The Centre wasn't really a tourist place, but it did sell tubs of ice-cream. They sat there, Katrina with Scottish Raspberry (exactly the same colour as her hoodie), Alex with Honeycomb, Clara with Tayberry and Archie with Vanilla. The ice-cream was soothing. Perhaps being in Scotland wasn't so bad.

'Tell us,' said Katrina, not wanting Uncle Archie to finish and get back to work, 'Tell us again about how you met.'

'This,' said Archie, 'was how I knew she was the lassie for me. It was when I was a student, travelling in Europe in the long summer break. I was waiting to go over this bridge near the border between France and Italy. I had never seen Clara before in my life. I was behind her in the queue, and I loved the way her hair, all curly, was glistening, full of gold lights. I can remember exactly the shade of blue her t-shirt was, because it was exactly the same colour as the sea loch on hot summer days. And although I was having a great time travelling, I suddenly felt both homesick and as though I was almost home – that loch is where I saw my first otter when I was a boy – maybe we'll see one there this summer. Anyway. She had a rucksack that was smaller than the ones most other people lugged about. I wondered how she did that. There's a limit to how light most people can travel.

'I could see a sketch book and a box of paints and a bundle of brushes and pencils strapped to the outside. Well, this queue snaked along, and up ahead was a kiosk where you had to pay a toll for the bridge. I remember seeing a board with pictures of all the ices and drinks you could buy. As we got closer I knew, I just knew, that this gorgeous lassie in front of me was going to buy this particular one, a watermelon one.'

'A granita,' Clara interjected. 'That's like a crunchy sorbet'. The twins knew this as they had heard the story before.

'It seemed that even though she was this wonderful mysterious stranger, I also knew everything there was to know about her. I still feel like that.'

This sounded strange but nice coming from Uncle Archie who was such a big man with such a deep Scottish voice. If you are like Uncle Archie, Alex thought, you don't have to pretend to be tough all the time. Alex couldn't imagine people laughing at Uncle Archie at school if, say, Uncle Archie still had to go to school and liked animals and was quiet and preferred drawing to fighting. But then Uncle Archie looked as though he'd be good at rugby and stuff like that.

'Anyway she got to the front of the queue, and I thought, now's my chance. She asked for her ticket and I leant over her shoulder and said: "And a watermelon ice too, and one for me as well". And she turned round and looked at me and smiled. Then we walked across the bridge and ate our ices together on the other side.'

'And here we are,' said Clara, 'still eating ice-cream together more than ten years later.'

Alex loved listening to this story, even though he never would have been the one to ask for it.

'I wish we knew stories like that about our mum and dad,' said Katrina. Alex gave a tiny nod of agreement. 'She doesn't like talking about him. Except sometimes to say cross things. All we know is his name and that he's a journalist, and that they met when she was on tour with the orchestra, and that he is somewhere in Russia.'

Alex got up and walked away. He started to throw pinecones as hard and far as he could, then started aiming for a branch high up in a Scots pine.

'He doesn't want to talk about things much either,' said Katrina, sounding very grown-up, as though she were the mum, or some kind outsider like a well-meaning teacher.

'It's very hard for you two,' said Clara. Archie jumped to his feet.

'Hey, Alex, see if you can hit that rock!' He took aim and lobbed a pinecone at a whitish boulder. He missed it by a whisker. So did Alex, but Katrina hit it first go. Alex rolled his eyes.

'Climbed any good trees lately?' Clara asked, coming to join them.

'Nah,' said Alex. 'We don't have that many good ones near us at home.'

'How about that one?' Clara pointed to one which had some pretty good starter branches. Alex was soon off and up it. Katrina chose another one about twenty metres away down the hill. She wouldn't have admitted that it looked a bit easier than Alex's. She had to go through the bracken and brambles to get there, but there was a tiny path. At the foot of the tree she stopped. There was something horrible up there. Flies buzzed around it. She screamed.

The others ran towards her. Something very dead was hanging in the branches.

'Oh, dear God,' said Clara, 'What is that?'

The heavy head lolled at a dreadful angle, the back legs and much of the body was gone, but you could see what it had been.

'A deer,' said Archie. 'But heaven knows how it got up there.'

Archie said he'd better clear it up, it was a relatively busy part of the forest, being just near the Visitor Centre. He walked with Clara and the twins back towards the car.

'I don't feel like going for a walk now,' said Katrina. 'Maybe we should go back and try ringing Mum again or something.'

'What will you do about the deer, though?' asked Alex, who was more interested than disgusted.

'I'll take a photo and then I guess I might haul it down and bury it. It's a bit of a hazard, and not exactly pretty.'

'Will you tell the police or something?' Alex went on.

'It's a dead deer in a forest. They'll not be that interested.'

'But isn't it a bit weird? How would it get up a tree?'

'I'm not sure, Alex.'

Chapter 9

They arrived home to find that someone, a boy with bright red hair, was sitting on the gate. He was bigger than the twins, but looked about their age. He was wearing faded jeans and a bright blue football shirt with red stripes that contrasted dramatically with his hair. Alex guessed it would be Inverness Caledonian Thistle who Uncle Archie supported.

'Huh,' said Katrina. 'What's he doing sitting on our gate?'

'That's Sandy,' said Clara. 'He's from the farm next door.' She didn't add that Sandy often sat on the gate, and in fact probably thought of it as pretty much being his gate to sit on, seeing as the fields surrounding the Carmichael's home all belonged to his family.

'Haven't you met him before? I suppose he's often helping on the farm. Maybe you can hang out together.'

The boy raised one freckly hand to say hi, and Clara stopped the car and rolled down the window.

'Hey, Sandy,' she said.

The boy gave a curt nod, more the sort of greeting that an old man would give.

'Me dad sent me over. Kimmy's had her pups. He wondered if Archie'd like one to replace Bobbie.'

'He might. That's really kind of you. I'll ask him tonight. How many did she have?'

'Five, and all doing well. Two's spoken for already, so he'd better say soon if he wants one.'

'Thanks. Would you like to come up and have a piece of cake? This is my nephew, Alex, and my niece, Katrina. They're staying for a while.'

Katrina smiled and said hi. Alex gave a nod as brief and grim as Sandy's.

'No thanks, Mrs. Carmichael. I've gotta get back.'

'Clara,' said Clara. She had been telling this boy to call her Clara for years.

With an air of importance aimed to make the twins feel like child passengers whilst he was someone with places to be, he pulled his bike off the hedge where he'd flung it and cycled away.

'Do you think you'll get a new dog? It would be so cool to get a puppy,' said Katrina.

'I'm sure Archie'll want one sooner or later. Maybe a girl this time. I suppose it wouldn't be for quite a few weeks if they've just been born. Mr. Tom would have settled in by then, or you'll be going home.'

'Sandy's a bit of a stupid name,' said Alex.

'Oh, do you think so? Do you know what it's short for?' Clara smiled.

'No.'

'Alexander. Lots of Scottish Alexanders are Sandy, in name and in looks.'

'Well I'm not Alexander, I'm Alexei.'

And nobody could have called his colouring sandy. The twins' hair was so deeply black that it could look almost bluey-green, like the magic feather from a magpie. Their eyes were a strange agate green.

'Would you like some cake?' Clara asked, once they were indoors and had found Mr. Tom sleeping on the kitchen windowsill.

'I'm still full from lunch, thanks,' said Alex.

'I feel a bit sick from that deer,' said Katrina.

'Sandy's nice, you know. You *could* hang out with him sometimes. He's the youngest of four. His brothers are all quite a bit older. I expect he'd be really glad of some company in the holidays.'

'He didn't seem very friendly,' said Katrina. Alex said nothing, he was too busy whispering to Mr. Tom.

'You could go with Archie when he goes to look at the puppies,' said Clara, ignoring her protests.

'Maybe.'

Clara looked in the pale blue enamel cake tin. Katrina loved the way that everything at Aunty Clara's was labelled – tea, coffee, flour, sugar, spaghetti, biscuits.

'When I'm grown-up I'm going to have an organised kitchen like you,' she said. Alex looked up. He felt a stab of longing for the tiny narrowboat where the bread (if there was any) lived in a tin from a huge pannetone that was completely the wrong shape for a breadbin. (He loved that Italian cake. He wished they could have it all year, not just at Christmas when the first violin from Mum's orchestra always gave them one.)

'Mum doesn't make cakes much,' he said.

'I find it really soothing, when things seem uncertain,' said Clara. 'It's so comforting knowing that if you add so much of one thing to so much of another and so much of something else you will definitely get something good, knowing that if you beat egg whites and fold in sugar and put it in the oven overnight, you'll have meringues in the morning. Not that I want to eat meringues in the morning.'

'Summer pudding though,' said Katrina.

'Yes, summer pudding in the morning is a different kettle of fish. We'll have to make some. We can go blackberrying. They're going to be early this year. But I'm going to make a cake this afternoon anyway, do you want to help?'

Katrina did. Alex had known that she would. He sometimes hated the way she seemed so at home in the world compared to him. And how could making a cake make anything better?

'Can I watch TV?' he asked. But there was nothing on. He trudged up the stairs to be by himself. He thought he'd read, but he fell asleep instead.

Alex woke to the smell of ginger cake wafting up the stairs, the sound of Katrina practising her flute, and his uncle's soft, deep voice calling him. He felt as though he'd been asleep for days, for centuries. He looked at the little clock. Five fifteen. He'd been

44

asleep for a few hours. He wondered what his mum was doing. Was she sleeping at the wrong times? Was she missing them? It was dreadful not even knowing what the place she was in was like. The Crescent Clinic. It sounded so clean and closed and clinic-ish – no, that wasn't the word – clinical. He knew what Katrina would say in her sensible voice: "At least we don't have to worry about where she is. At least she'll be safe and getting better." But he was worrying.

He sat up. His feet found the soft woolly mat beside the bed. He was desperately thirsty. He went downstairs.

'I've been reading,' he said, embarrassed about sleeping in the day like a little kid who needed a nap. Aunty Clara smiled. Uncle Archie gave him a hug. He put up with it for a moment – it was quite nice – but then he shrugged Archie off.

Alex gulped down his apple juice and Clara poured him some more and gently pushed a dotty blue plate with a wedge of ginger cake towards him. Katrina had put away her flute and was sipping tea. Alex suspected that she was just pretending to like it so that she seemed grown-up. He ignored her.

'What did you do with the deer?' he asked.

'Well,' said Archie, taking a big glug of tea. 'It was very strange. I got caught up with some walkers who had a flat battery, needed a jump start, then they managed to reverse into a ditch and needed a tow out. Then my old boss dropped in for a chat and a cup of tea. When I finally went back to the tree sort it out, it was gone. Just disappeared. Wondered if I'd imagined the whole thing. Saved me an unpleasant job, but it was very strange.'

45

'But where did it go? How did it get up there?' Alex asked. 'Deer don't jump into trees. Apart from those ones in Africa that eat high-up leaves.'

'Maybe something was chasing it and it got stuck. It's not the rutting season, is it?' said Katrina.

'And dead deer can't jump down,' said Alex.

'Can we forget about it for the moment? I'm trying to eat this lovely cake,' said Archie.

'Oh, I forgot to tell you,' said Clara, cutting second wodges for everybody, 'Sandy McPherson came over. They have puppies and wondered if you wanted one.'

'Aye, I might. Maybe it's time,' Archie said, looking over at the rug where Bobbie should have been. 'Maybe it's time. I'll have a shower and the twins can come with me and help me pick.'

'You'd better go tonight,' said Clara. 'Two are taken already. I haven't done any work today. Why don't you drive down to the beach afterwards and get some chips for supper?'

Chapter 10

The McPherson's farm covered a thousand acres. The twins were glad to be going in Archie's Land Rover. They had the feeling that Sandy McPherson was already looking down his freckly turned-up nose at them.

They drove up a long drive, which seemed very grand, and ended at a solid-looking redbrick farmhouse. There were five large windows peering down at them from the second floor, four on the ground floor and a shiny green door. You could see lots of chimneys and what must have been the little windows of attic bedrooms too. A black Alsatian and a collie who looked quite like Archie's old Bobbie came running out, barking a warning or a greeting, depending how you looked at it. The dogs were followed by Sandy McPherson. He yelled 'Quiet! Heel!' and the dogs were silent.

'Hi, Mr. Carmichael,' he said and nodded at the twins who nodded back.

'Hear you've got some puppies,' said Archie. 'Can we take a look?'

'They're in the back kitchen,' said Sandy and he led them around the side of the house, past what looked like a back door, to the rear of the house where there was *another* back door.

How many doors do these people need? Alex wondered, thinking of The Bluebell, which had only a hatch really, and nothing that looked like even a front door. At home in London, they had to collect their mail from a lockable box in a bank of such boxes. It was a job that both he and Katrina liked, even though there wasn't usually much to collect. Once they had thrown a bill in the river, thinking it would help. It had floated right up to The Bluebell and their mum had spotted it. Luckily she had thought that it was funny, though she said it wouldn't help to throw bills in The Thames, it would only get them into trouble if they were late in paying. Plus, she said, there was always the possibility that they might be throwing away a cheque. Alex and Katrina wouldn't have admitted that they were secretly hoping for something from their dad. Very occasionally he sent them postcards from where he was working. They kept them safe, though sometimes they both felt like throwing them in the river too.

Anyway, they followed Sandy McPherson through this back, back door and along a passageway, passing long queues of the sort of posh wellies that have buckles on, through a wooden door with a latch like the ones at Aunty Clara's, and into a warm kitchen. 'The back kitchen', Alex thought. Meaning that these people had more than one. Why would anybody need more than one kitchen?

A sharp-faced woman with the same red hair as Sandy was using a mallet to bash a steak. There were five other steaks, already bashed, spread out on a huge marble slab, dripping blood. She looked up and gave the visitors a rather menacing smile. The full strength of its beam was directed at Archie.

'Oh, I'm sorry,' said Archie in the gentle voice that the twins loved so much. 'I thought you'd have had your tea by now.'

The woman gave a few more bashes and pushed a few strands of her red hair away from her eyes. Her fingers were streaked with blood and the twins looked in horror at the smudges she left on her forehead.

'It's no problem, Archie. I've just got to flash fry these, everybody likes them nice and rare. You don't get tired of steak, even when it's your livelihood. The rest's done,' she said, nodding towards the big crimson aga. You could almost see the smells of things, probably potatoes with rosemary and some sort of pudding, coming from it.

They are just the sort of people, Alex thought, who would have home-made puddings, apple pies or crumbles, or something with a stupid name like spotted dick or upside-down turnover every single day. It wasn't fair.

'These are my nephew and niece,' Archie said. 'Alex and Katrina McCloud.'

'Good Scottish names,' said Mrs. McPherson.

'Mine's Russian actually,' said Alex.

'Fancy! And you do look like two little Russians.'

49

Katrina had attempted a smile, but her face was now set in a neutral position. She knew what Mrs McPherson was thinking. Sooner or later, people as old as Mrs McPherson always said something about Petrova Fossil in *Ballet Shoes*. Katrina was sure that they were always thinking of the bit when Petrova arrives and they say she is a "sallow" baby, and Nana says "Well, I know who's going to be Miss Plain in my nursery."

Archie had never seen Alex look so fierce. He couldn't think why. Here they were with perfectly nice Mrs McPherson, about to see some puppies, and with young Sandy McPherson as a potential friend for the summer...

'You take them through and show them, Sandy,' Mrs McPherson went on. 'Your dad and brothers will be back soon, wanting their dinner.'

Katrina and Alex exchanged glances. It sounded like the bit in *Jack and the Beanstalk* when the giant was expected home.

'This way,' said Sandy, indicating another door, this one small and pointy like one in a church.

The door opened into another kitchen. The cooker and sink looked unused. Instead of a table in the centre of the room there was a huge basket, a very tired-looking Border collie, and five gorgeous puppies.

'Oh!' said Alex and Katrina with one voice, and they fell to their knees. Uncle Archie crouched down beside them.

The mother dog looked up rather mournfully.

'Don't pick 'em up till she's used to you,' said Sandy.

They spoke gently to Kimmy and told her how clever she was, and she didn't mind at all when, a little later, they each picked up one of the sleepy bundles of fur. Katrina didn't know why, but she felt like crying when she held the squirmy, soft little thing.

'Choose this one, Uncle Archie, it looks like it has a star on its head.'

'No, this one,' said Alex. 'It has giant paws so it will be really strong.'

'That one's spoken for,' said Sandy.

'I'll take the star one then, if it's a girl,' said Archie. 'But I'm sure they'll all be fine dogs.'

'You can come and visit her whenever you want 'til she's ready,' said Sandy. And he smiled at the twins properly for the first time.

The sound and smell of steak frying was creeping under the door, and they heard angry deep voices.

'Think me dad's back,' said Sandy. 'It'll be our dinner.'

'We'll be away then, come on twins, thanks Sandy. They're grand puppies,' said Archie.

A huge man was sitting at the table in the kitchen, alongside two giant versions of Sandy.

'Where's Bill?' asked Sandy.

'Outside in the barn. We had to get the vet to one of the heifers.'

'What's up, Dad? Shall I go and help?'

'You'll see. Deep cuts on the rump and hind legs.'

'Sorry to hear that,' said Archie.

'Who'd be a farmer?' said Mr. McPherson, as a huge dish of potatoes appeared in front of him.

'Aye, Jim McIntyre lost another sheep to dogs last week. Haven't heard if they've caught the culprits,' Archie told him.

'Aye, but this couldn't be dogs. Too deep. Looks like someone attacked him with a handful of knives.'

'Oh, that's horrible!' said Katrina. The McPhersons all slowly nodded their agreement.

'Sandy, see Mr. Carmichael out, and then go and find out if the vet's done,' said Mrs McPherson, sliding the third of the steaks onto a plate.

'I hope they'll get to the bottom of this,' said Archie. 'And they're grand pups. I'll definitely take one. Thanks.'

Outside they saw Ed Stirling, the vet, stowing his bag in the back of his van.

'Ed!' Archie called. 'How's it going? You remember my niece and nephew, Katrina and Alex? They're up for the holidays.'

'Hello,' said Ed, with smile that seemed much more friendly than the standard local greeting, and an Edinburgh accent that the twins found easier to understand than the McPherson's Highland. 'Been to see the pups? I looked in yesterday. Still doing well are they?'

'They're grand,' said Archie.

'Uncle Archie's going to have the one with the star on its head,' said Alex.

The vet smiled again.

'Is the heifer ok? Will it die?' Katrina asked.

'No.' Ed Stirling shook his head and smiled again. 'Some nasty cuts though. Very deep. Could be wire, hard to say. Maybe one of the McPherson lads left something lying about and didn't want to say. And do you still want to be a vet, Katrina?' She smiled and nodded.

'You could come out with me one day if you like, you too, Alex,' he said.

'Yes, please!' said Katrina, grinning.

'I'll give your aunty a ring, then. Where are you all off to?'

'Chippy,' said Archie. 'We haven't had our tea yet. Want to join us?'

'Still got two more calls to make. Let's go for a pint soon.'

The kind sun warms her. Dark velvet absorbs the rays. No cave or dank den for her today. Instead, high on the rocky hill, she stretches and basks. Below her the water glitters, a distant disc of blue. Last night she lost her prey, it was too big. But this morning she fed – a young deer – tender and good. Her belly is full. So now she stretches, basks, dozes, no more than a shadow on a flat grey rock.

'I hate this summer,' Katrina said, as they drove back down the McPherson's long drive. 'I mean, I don't want to be rude, I like staying with you and being in Scotland, but whenever everything seems ok, or that it might be getting better, something horrible happens. It's as though the world is laughing at us. And of course, Mum…'

'Ach, Katrina,' said Archie. He would have hugged her if he hadn't been driving.

'In London,' Katrina went on, 'it was nearly the end of term, and everything was meant to be fun with the Year 6 party and all that, and then suddenly Mum goes off and it's really scary. And then we come up here, and Mum's in the clinic so she should be getting better, but we aren't allowed to talk to her, and we go for a picnic and it should be lovely, and then there's a dead deer in a tree. And then we come and see some really cute puppies, and it's so cool that you are going to get one, and then we find out that someone has attacked a poor defenceless heifer…' Katrina rubbed furiously at her eyes, making them look redder and sorer than if she'd just let the tears fall.

'Ach, Katrina. Things aren't really that bad. It's just the countryside, and farming, and bad luck. Your mum will soon be better.' Katrina gave a big sniff and tried to smile. 'And the heifer will be ok. They're hardly defenceless,' said Archie.

Alex reached over and patted his sister on the arm.

'Then how did something manage to attack it like that?' he asked.

Archie gave a slight shrug, and said nothing for a while. They took the road that led down to the village and parked by the loch.

'Some chips'll cheer us up,' said Archie. 'We'll go and eat by the water.'

'Yeah, cheer up, Katrina. We might see an otter,' said Alex.

'We'd be lucky to here. Usually too busy for anything really wild,' said Archie.

Uncle Archie was right about the chips. They were perfect. Golden and salty with just the right combination of fat ones and crispy ones. He had a piece of fish too. They sat at one of the picnic tables by the loch and ate them using the little wooden forks that Katrina and Alex loved. London chip shops didn't seem to give them out anymore.

'This is the second time we've had chip shop chips in a week,' said Katrina, as Alex passed her another sachet of ketchup. Uncle Archie was really cool about things like sachets of ketchup. He'd always buy plenty. It wasn't true, thought Katrina, that Scots were mean. Uncle Archie definitely wasn't mean. Why did people make jokes about that? 'Less than a week ago we were in London and Mum was lost,' said Katrina.

Alex noticed that the chips seemed to have restored her annoying grown-upishness. They were delicious, but suddenly he didn't want any more.

Although it was now nearly eight o'clock, it was hardly getting dark. The water in the loch, though, looked deeply indigo. It could be that colour on the brightest of days. It was as though the loch obeyed its own set of rules about light and reflection, or had its own sort of anti-light that came from its depths.

'Do people *ever* swim in the loch?' Alex asked. He had seen plenty of fishermen, and they had sometimes paddled, but he couldn't remember seeing anyone swimming.

'This is water from when the glaciers retreated, and it hasn't warmed up much since then,' said Archie. 'They'd have to be brave.'

'I might,' said Katrina. She was a bold swimmer who would always plunge straight in whilst her mum and Alex took tentative little steps.

'Only if Clara or I am with you. There can be dangerous currents, even in a loch. You have to remember how deep it is in parts. This is quite a body of water.'

'Ok, Uncle Archie.' Katrina smiled and slipped her rather greasy hand into his.

55

Alex watched the little waves breaking on the shore. You could tell the water was cold just by looking at it. He remembered paddling here with Aunty Clara and Mum last summer. Some of the stones had been green and really slippery, and things glinted with false promises amongst the pebbles. You'd think you had spotted some money and it would be a ring-pull, or you might think you could see some piece of treasure, some lost jewellery, and it would turn out to be a vicious fishhook. If Katrina was going to swim, he might just sit and draw, or go beachcombing, lochcombing he supposed you should call it, or just skim stones. He'd be happy doing that for hours. Or maybe they would go to the big pool in Inverness one day. Or to the proper beach somewhere.

When they were eight they'd gone on holiday to St. Malo in France with mum and some of the orchestra people. He'd loved that. Mum had been happy all the time.

'You had enough, Alex?' Uncle Archie interrupted his daydream.

Alex looked down at the chips (which were now cold, greasy and flaccid) and nodded. Uncle Archie scrumpled up the paper, and they dropped all the detritus of their dinner into the bin in the tiny car park. Theirs was the only car there (if you can call a forest ranger's Land Rover a car) though there was a VW camper van, a really cool one that looked as though it belonged to some surfers, but there was no sign of them. Alex wished that he had a van like that. He wouldn't need anything or anyone else. He'd drive so far away, he'd just keep driving and driving, and nobody would ever know where he was.

Aunty Clara was sitting on the bench under the big oak tree when they got back. She was making quick watercolour sketches of her chickens as they pecked about her feet. Dusk was approaching and the hens would soon be putting themselves to bed. Clara looked up and then back down at her work. She gave it a quizzical look and then put her brush down. Alex had the feeling that she had hoped they'd be gone a little longer.

'Your mum phoned. She sounded quite a bit better. She sent lots of love,' said Clara.

'Oh no! We missed her!' said Katrina. 'Can we ring her back?'

'We can try.'

They all went into the cottage and Clara dialed the number. They stood and watched her.

'It's ringing.' It rang and rang. 'Perhaps they don't have many people there in the evenings to answer the phone.'

Alex saw Archie raise his eyebrows and head off towards the kitchen.

'It's still ringing.' said Clara. 'I'll – oh! Oh, hello, could I possibly talk to Chrissie McCloud? I'm her sister. I have her children with me and they'd like to say hello.'

The twins could hear what sounded like a telephone voice in a cartoon going 'Wa waw wa waw wa'. Aunty Clara held the phone slightly away from her ear.

'Oh, ok. Please could you tell her that we rang. We'll try again tomorrow.'

She put the phone down. Katrina saw Alex's eyes brimful.

'Sorry, twins. She's in some sort of session, and they won't disturb her.'

.

They heard Archie go 'huh' in the kitchen. 'These sessions are important. They are the way they get better. They have to talk about their troubles,' said Clara.

Alex and Katrina had been inside clinics and hospitals when their mum had been ill before. They had seen into rooms where adults sat in circles, rolling cigarettes and talking about their problems. They had seen the mismatched chairs and the way people didn't seem to be looking at each other. Alex had never forgotten one big grizzled man, like a wounded bear, who had started crying when Katrina had offered him one of her cough sweets.

Why on earth would grown-ups, who could go anywhere in the world and do whatever they liked, go to one of those places? They must be stupid, really stupid.

'Where's Mr. Tom?' he said.

'He's been asleep on your bed for hours,' said Aunty Clara. 'He's much more settled. We could think about letting him out to explore soon if you wanted.'

'Not yet,' said Alex. 'I don't want him to go off and get lost too.'

'I agree. Keep him in for a while longer,' said Uncle Archie, glancing out to where the darkness was falling over the forest.

Katrina was reading under the patchwork quilt whilst Alex sat drawing on the end of her bed. Aunty Clara came up to say goodnight.

'Are you two ok?' she asked. Alex shrugged.

'Kind of,' said Katrina.

'I know it's really tough, but things will get better. Your mum will be better soon. You have to remember it's an illness, a disease. She will get better. Try to think about the good times as well, the happy times. Those times will be back.'

'Will they?' mumbled Alex.

'Of course they will,' Clara said. She patted Katrina's legs under the quilt then put her arm around Alex's shoulders. He stiffened, but after a while relaxed into the hug. 'I know life is really hard at the moment, but it won't always be like this. Before you go to sleep, try to make a list, on paper or just in your head, of good times, happy memories.' She hugged Katrina too and went back down the stairs. When she was out of earshot, Alex said:

'Like that will help.'

'We might as well try,' said Katrina. 'That time in France, swimming in the sea in the rain.' Alex gave a little nod, but said nothing. 'When we got Mr Tom and he was so tiny he could fit in my pencil case,' Katrina went on. Alex put his sketchbook down and thought for a moment.

'Those swingboats,' he said.

'Us up one end and Mum at the other – we had so many goes,' said Katrina. They could see their mum laughing, her hair blowing about as they swung higher and higher. 'She loves carousels too.'

'Always chooses the horse with the stupidest name, like Trevor,' said Alex. 'And she's really good at fixing stuff on the boat. Not many people could do all the stuff she does for The Bluebell.'

'She does the best birthdays,' said Katrina.

'Remember when she caught that duck with the plastic around its leg? She can do loads of things that other mums can't do,' said Alex.

'She definitely isn't like other mums,' said Katrina. Alex nodded and gave a sad little half-smile.

Chapter 11

Ed Stirling rang the next afternoon. Would the twins like to come out on a few visits with him that afternoon? He would pick them up at three. Alex didn't want to go, so it was only Katrina who sat and waited on the gate for Ed to arrive.

The first visit was to a cat with some kittens. There were five of them, three ginger and two tortoiseshell. They were so new that Katrina was only allowed to hold each one for a moment after Ed had checked it over. He had some regular blood tests to do on some cows at the next farm, and then they went on a visit to a riding stables where one of the horses was a bit lame. The final visit was back in the village by the loch to a Mrs. McGraw and her vicious Westie, Minnie.

Minnie McGraw was the smallest, but the most formidable dog on Ed Stirling's books. She was feared by local children and adults alike. Unfortunately she was often in need of the vet. Her extreme greed and ability to ingest, but not to digest the inedible had led to many emergency and after hours call-outs. In the last few months Ed had treated her for the effects of eating a dead seagull, some car keys, and Mrs. McGraw's great nephew's packed lunch – not just the crisps, sandwiches, apple and chewy bar, but all the foil and packaging too. He wondered what it would be today. Mrs. McGraw liked to go along by the loch, where Minnie could terrorise tourists and their dogs. (Locals who saw them coming knew to skidaddle.) The problem was that Mrs. McGraw was pretty old and immobile, so she let Minnie wander off for long periods by herself, whilst she travelled in splendour along the road on her motorised ride-on-thingy, Ed couldn't remember what you called them. If they had lived at Loch Ness, Ed thought, there would definitely have been no Loch Ness monster. Minnie would have eaten it by now.

Ed knocked loudly on the cottage door and waited. And waited. And waited. Perhaps they were out. Perhaps Minnie had thrown up whatever it was already and they'd set off in search of something else.

No such luck.

He heard the shuffle of Mrs McGraw's slippers, but no signature snarl or yapping from Minnie. Not a good sign. The door opened and there was Mrs. McGraw, almost as wide as her hallway.

'Ooh, thank goodness you've come at last! I'm so worried about my wee Minnie.'

'Hello Mrs McGraw. I've got my new assistant with me today. This is Katrina McCloud, she's Clara and Archie's niece. Is that ok?'

'You come on in, hen.' Katrina smiled and said thank you.

'Where's the patient?' asked Ed. 'What do you think she's eaten this time?'

'She's not eaten anything. She's under the sideboard trembling and I cannae get her out. She's been there for hours and she's missed her tea.'

'Oh dear,' said Ed, smiling in what he hoped was a reassuring way. 'Don't worry. I'm sure we can get her out.'

Ed and Katrina followed Mrs. McGraw down the hall and into her dining room. Here there was a table and four chairs, but most of the space was taken up by a sideboard – a hulking great piece of oak. It was covered with ornaments – simpering shepherdesses whose features and costumes seemed designed to trap dust, a collection of ceramic dogs (none of them had quite the vicious glint in their eye, or the menacing under-bite and protruding teeth that Minnie possessed), and photos of Mrs. McGraw's many relatives, none of whom visited very often.

Ed and Katrina crouched down and looked underneath it.

'Watch out, Katrina,' Ed whispered, 'Minnie might go for you.' There were clumps of fluff and fur, chewed doggy toys, a few long, oily, bedraggled feathers (the very last of that seagull?) and something grey that could have been a pair of the late Mr. McGraw's underpants. Ed Stirling was used to reaching into some pretty odd places. Minnie was there in the corner, trembling, and whimpered when she saw them peering at her.

'It's alright, there's a good girl, let's get you out of there,' he said softly. He slowly extended one arm and stroked Minnie gently on the back of her wiry little head. Minnie made a whining noise. She didn't even snarl. But the sideboard was so big and the gap underneath it so small that with his huge shoulders and arms, Ed couldn't reach enough to get her out. 'Hmm, I'm just too big. Do you want to try, Katrina? If she looks like she might snap, leave her alone.'

Katrina lay on the floor. She could easily slide her arm under the dresser and reach Minnie.

'Hey, Minnie,' she said softly. 'Don't worry, it's ok, we'll soon get you out.' She began to stroke the back of Minnie's head.

'Give her one of these treats,' said Mrs McGraw. Katrina heard the box rattling and then one of Ed's big hands slid a couple of the little biscuit bones towards her.

'Hey, Minnie, we've got your favourites,' said Katrina, offering them to her. Minnie looked at them for a moment and then gobbled them up. 'See, girl, everything's alright. Come on, there's a good girl.' Katrina gently scooped Minnie up and started to pull her out. For a moment Minnie tried to resist, her claws caught in the artificial fibres of the carpet, and she whimpered again; but with firm and gentle hands, Katrina soon had her out. She stood up, cuddling Minnie and passed her to Ed. Minnie nuzzled into his shirt, more frightened kitten than vicious terrier.

'Well done, Katrina, nice work!' said Ed.

'Clever lass!' said Mrs McGraw.

'Let's get Minnie calmed down and take a look at her,' said Ed. He ran his hands over the dog, who seemed to relax in his expert care. Minnie even let him look in her mouth and ears. 'Well, there don't seem to be any surface wounds – everything looks and feels physically ok. But she does seem to have had a nasty scare. What happened? Might she have been in a fight?' Minnie whimpered again. This wasn't the Minnie he knew. She seemed like a different dog. Could somebody have swapped her for another one? He took a surreptitious look at the collar. No, it said "Minnie. 12 Waterside Cottages" and the phone number. And who in the world would want to take Minnie anyway? He took Minnie's temperature. (Around normal.) He shifted his attention to Mrs McGraw who had lowered herself into one of the dining room chairs. 'Here, you take her now.' He settled Minnie in Mrs McGraw's ample lap. Katrina knelt down and stroked Minnie too.

'You're a natural, Katrina,' said Ed.

'Aye,' said Mrs McGraw, 'Minnie doesn't usually let strangers near her.'

'So how did this all start?'

'Well,' Mrs McGraw began, 'we were out this morning nice and early, just taking our usual walk along by the loch. I was waiting on my scooter,' (Ah, thought Ed, that's what they called it, a mobility scooter.) Minnie was having her wee sniff around on the pebbles. She had disappeared off behind those big boulders down at the far end, she likes it down there near the stream.' Ed and Katrina smiled and nodded. Minnie was calmer now.

'I was chatting away to Mrs Armstrong, she was telling me all about what's been going on at the school this last year, she's a dinner lady.'

'I know Mrs Armstrong, magnificent tabby,' said Ed.

'Then Minnie came bolting back. I've never seen her like that before. Her ears were flat, her tail was down, the wee thing was trying to disappear. She fair threw herself into my lap, wouldn't stop shaking, so I turned the scooter around and we came straight home. Something must have scared her. Mrs. Armstrong said she'd never seen anything move that fast.'

'Well, something certainly seems to have spooked her. Physically she seems fine. Maybe she disturbed an otter and it went for her. Friend of mine lost a finger to an injured otter.'

'She's a brave little girl,' said Mrs. McGraw, 'not easily frightened.'

'I know,' said Ed. 'She's a tough little thing. I'm sure she'll be alright soon. I'd keep her confined to the house and your garden for a day or so, see how she does, maybe keep her on the lead the next time you go out. Can you manage that with your scooter?'

'Aye, we'll manage that.'

'I'd better be off. Call me if she doesn't settle back to normal. You stay there with her. We'll see ourselves out.'

Minnie was now meekly curled up, half-buried in her mistress's itchy-looking skirt.

'Thank you, Ed. You're a kind lad. Thank you, Katrina.'

'By the way, was there anyone else down there?' asked Ed. 'Any tourists? Strange dogs? There's been some sheep-worrying too. Maybe there's an out-of-control dog or something in the area…'

'There wasn't a soul,' said Mrs. McGraw. 'Not a soul.' Ed Stirling was careful to close the door firmly behind them.

'That's it for the day, Katrina. Think I'll take a look down by those boulders on the beach, sometime, see if there was an otter family. An adult otter would be even fiercer than Minnie if some cubs were under threat.'

'Can we go now?' asked Katrina.

'Sorry. I said I'd get you back for your tea. Another time.'

'Ok,' said Katrina, gazing at the loch as they drove past. 'I would love to see an otter, or whatever it was.'

Chapter 12

Aunty Clara gave Alex some of her books about drawing to read that night.

'This,' she said, passing him a large floppy one, 'was what really got me started. I was given it when I was about your age.' Alex read *How To Draw Animals* by Walter Foster. Price U.S.A. $2. It was a bit smaller than A3 and had a creased yellowish-brown cover with an impressive drawing of a monkey and her baby. It looked really old.

'I wish I could draw like that,' he said.

'You will. It's all about looking, and looking, and then looking some more. You look at the light and the textures and the shadows. You look at what lies beneath the skin, the muscles especially. What's underneath can be as important as what you see on the surface. That's why some of the great artists have been anatomists, dissecting bodies, even the bodies of horses, to understand how they work, why they look the way they do. When I was at art school...'

'What, like that cow cut in half and that dead shark in a tank? We saw those on a school trip. Someone was sick, but I think that was from too much Banana Yazoo.'

'Eugh. But these anatomical drawings are much better than Damien Hirst's work. Those artists were pioneers, examining the muscles and the tendons scientifically.'

'Have you got books of those?'

'Oh, probably, somewhere – they aren't really bedtime reading.'

'I don't mind things that other people think are disgusting,' said Alex.

'Well just look at Walter Foster tonight anyway,' Clara said, backing out of the room. Katrina was already asleep. She'd had a nice hot bath and been overcome by tiredness. Clara thought it was a healthy reaction, much better to sleep if you were stressed or upset by something. Alex didn't seem sleepy at all now. He looked as though he would be reading and drawing for half the night.

Alex sat in bed looking at the book. It made it seem so easy. You started by thinking about the basic shapes that a creature was made of, the intersecting circles and ovals of a cat for instance; you started with those and worked up from that.

Before he'd always started with outlines, or started with the head, or one front paw, and then carried on from there. The trouble with his old method though was that the proportions never came out right. With this new "looking at the shapes" method you'd get the proportions before anything else happened.

He flicked through the book. On the back page it said that there were 167 other books in the series. He wondered if you could still get them. They were all by people with really cool, crazy names. Alexei McCloud was nothing compared to Merlin Enabnit, Hellen Lion, Dixi Hall, Mannie Gonsalves, Eugene M. Frandzen or Walter J. Wilwerding. Some of the books on Chinese painting were by "The Chows". He would have loved *How To Draw Horses* or *Around The World and Then Some* by Walter Foster, or *Art Secrets and Shortcuts (all colour)* by Fritz Willis. Some of his mum's music books were really old. You could probably get really old art books too, or maybe a library would have them back home. If they ever went back. At the moment it all seemed so far away. Scotland was ok, Aunty Clara and Uncle Archie were ok, but he couldn't help missing The Bluebell. He hoped it was alright. At least Pippa and Brian had said they would look after it. You could trust Pippa and Brian. He could imagine them going every day and watering the plants, and maybe sitting and having a cup of tea so that it looked as though someone was living there. He wished he'd stayed in London. They shouldn't have told Aunty Clara. Couldn't they have just stayed there by themselves? They managed pretty much by themselves anyway, even when Mum was around. It wasn't as though Aunty Clara had actually done much. The police had found Mum, and the hospital had sorted out about the clinic. If only they'd just kept quiet. He hoped no other cat tried to take over the territory whilst Mr. Tom was away.

Alex sometimes thought that Mr. Tom could see his thoughts. This was one of those times. Mr. Tom appeared. He marched into the room with his tail proudly in the air, and with one bound was on Alex's pillow. He took up all the space. Now Alex couldn't decide whether to use the method to try drawing the tiger, or to have a go at drawing Mr. Tom from real life.

'You're bigger and better than a pillow, aren't you Mr. Tom,' Alex whispered into the soft marmalade fur. 'Shall I draw you or a tiger? You're better than a tiger...'

Mr. Tom purred – he clearly agreed – and went to sleep.

It was hard to see the circles and ovals that were supposed to make up a huge ginger tom. Mr. Tom looked more like a big box, a shoe box with legs. Alex was suddenly very tired. He pushed the book to one side and put his head down in the small space that was left between Mr. Tom and the wall. He thought he would close his eyes for a minute and think about how he would do the drawing. Aunty Clara had said that you had to look and look and look. He thought that you could sort of look at things with your eyes closed. He had pictures in his head of Mr. Tom doing different things, leaping with his body all stretched out, sitting neatly when he was quiet, but not asleep, in a position that made him look like a hen sitting on her eggs, marching in with his tail in the air, looking fierce and all fluffed up when he had to see off the evil marauding tabby from five boats down...

There were footsteps on the stairs up to the attic, heavy footsteps that were trying not to be. Uncle Archie. Alex was too tired to open his eyes. He heard the lamp click off and the heavy footsteps (trying not to be) retreat down the stairs. He was still going to do that drawing. He wasn't really falling asleep. He was just going to stay still with his eyes shut for a minute. He wasn't really falling asleep.

He heard something. It was almost like hearing a feeling. He sat straight up in bed. The only light was coming through the curtains – bright moonlight. He knew that he had heard something, but that it was something almost silent. Mr. Tom had heard it too. He was awake and alert, but frozen, his ears pricked up, the fur along his back and his tail half-fluffed up. The thing they had heard was outside. Alex crept out of bed; some instinct told him that he must be completely silent. He carefully pushed some of the soft fabric of the curtains to one side. He knew that he mustn't even let the curtain rings knock together. And then he saw it. It was a dark shape, an outline, sitting on the low roof of Aunty Clara's studio. It was the outline of a cat, a huge dark cat, much bigger than any normal cat.

Alex looked and looked, fixing the image in his mind, hardly able to believe what he was seeing.

Fur brushing his bare arm almost startled him. Mr. Tom jumped onto the windowsill and looked out – only for a micro-second – then hissed and leapt away. Alex turned to see Mr. Tom burrowing under the quilt. He looked back outside. The other cat was gone.

What should he do? He could go outside with a torch and try to see it again. He had a feeling it would be long gone though, it had vanished instantly. And what would he do? Go 'Here kitty, here kitty...' to a creature that might be a giant Scottish wild cat, or a panther or a lioness or something? He wasn't scared. He was interested. He could wake up Katrina (but she was so difficult to wake up and would be grumpy) or Uncle Archie or Aunty Clara.

But they'd just say that he had been dreaming or think that he was making it up because he was upset about Mum. He carried on looking and looking until his feet were so cold that he could hardly move them and his elbows ached from leaning on the windowsill. There was nothing there. He could see so much more now that his eyes were used to the moonlit darkness – the outlines of the other buildings, the henhouse, the tree with the tyre swing, Uncle Archie's Land Rover and Aunty Clara's little Renault beside it, the trees at the end of the garden where the forest began and stretched off into the Highland distance, towards the loch and then the mountains. The creature could be anywhere now.

He limped back to bed, his feet still numb, and moved the drawing books and pencils onto the floor. He could sort them out in the morning. He snuggled under the covers, hoping to get warm again. The bundle of fur that was Mr. Tom was in the space where his feet wanted to go. Mr. Tom never normally went that deep down in a bed. Even Mr. Tom's fur felt colder than normal, the way it did when he was ill.

Alex fell back to sleep thinking about what he had seen. A big cat had been there, on the roof of Aunty Clara's studio. He knew that it had been there. He didn't know whether anyone would believe him.

Alex woke up before anyone else the next morning. He tiptoed down the stairs, stuck his bare feet into his trainers, and went outside. He wondered if he should let the hens out. Aunty Clara normally got up pretty early to let them out. He supposed she would be up soon. But what if he let them out and the creature was lying in wait? What if it was lying in wait for him? He smiled at the thought, but he still went back in and put on Uncle Archie's waxed jacked. It was huge and weighed a ton and hung down below his knees, but it would be just what he needed if the creature were a mountain lion. He could remember exactly what to do from *The Worst Case Scenario Handbook*:

"Upon sighting a mountain lion, do not run. Do not crouch down. Try to make yourself appear larger by opening wide your coat."

He decided to take Aunty Clara's big umbrella too, just in case. Plus it would be useful for poking into bushes. He reluctantly closed the door behind him. He would have liked to leave it open in case he needed to sprint back inside, but they were still keeping Mr. Tom shut in.

He began to circumnavigate the house, looking for any evidence of the cat, some strands of fur caught in a bush or paw prints, disturbed plants where it might have passed through or lurked in the flower beds. There was nothing. He made it to Aunty Clara's studio and looked up at where it had been. Nothing. There was gravel along the side of the building. He looked to see if it had been disturbed. It wasn't smooth, but you couldn't really tell anything by that. Clara and Archie weren't the sort of people who bothered about having flat gravel. Alex remembered going on a school trip to a castle. The whole class had been told off for making patterns with their feet in the gravel on the grand drive where the coach had dropped them off.

'Somebody has to rake that every day to keep it looking nice and smooth!' the teacher had yelled, and then, when some of them had tried to smooth it out, they'd been told off even more.

'Your parents won't be pleased to see you coming home with mud and dust all over your school shoes!' His mum was too cool to care about mud or dust, and anyway he didn't have school shoes, only trainers.

Well, the creature (Alex was almost starting to wonder what it was now) hadn't mucked up the gravel; but then maybe it had leapt and landed straight on the grass instead. He thought about what Mr. Tom would do. He pictured him sitting up on the studio roof. He would be much smaller than that creature. He imagined how Mr. Tom would get down from there. He wouldn't leap – he would sort of pour himself down the wall. If he did that, he would probably land in the gravel. Alex looked harder at the gravel. You really couldn't tell a thing, and perhaps a bigger creature would land further away from the wall. And what about sounds? He hadn't heard anything when the creature had vanished. But would he have? And what was it that had woken him up? He tried to remember. Had he been asleep or still awake? Something had made him get up and go to the window, and something had really freaked out Mr. Tom. What had done that?

Suddenly he sensed movement behind him, heard crunching on the stones, he spun around, making himself huge with the jacket. It was Aunty Clara.

She smiled down at him.

'What is it, Alex?'

'Last night,' he said. 'Last night, I heard something land on silent feet.' She looked a bit startled.

'Something land on silent feet?'

'I'm looking for it now. It had the shape of a big cat. Like a leopard or a panther or a mountain lion. It was on the roof of your studio. I saw it in the night. It was a shadow in the dark, sitting up there, and Mr. Tom saw it too, and he hissed and hid, and that made me look away. And when I looked back, it was gone.'

'Oh,' said Aunty Clara, looking perplexed.

'I'm just looking for it, or any paw prints or anything...and I don't think you should let your hens out. It isn't safe.'

'Alex, they have to come out every morning. They can't stay in the dark all day. They'd be miserable. They have to come out to eat and drink and peck about.'

'I'm not making this up. I saw a big creature and it might be dangerous.'

'Perhaps it was a dream you had. They can be really vivid if you're worried about things.'

Alex rolled his eyes.

'It was not a dream. I'm not worried about things.'

'Well,' said Aunty Clara, slowly, as though she were explaining something to a toddler, 'if it wasn't a dream then you shouldn't be out here either, even if you have got my umbrella and Archie's coat.'

'Sorry about that. But, do you know what you're meant to do if a mountain lion's going to pounce? Make yourself as big as possible, like this, and make a really big noise.' He held out the coat again as though he was making wings and pulled himself up as tall as he could. 'They probably won't attack if they think you are that big. They don't understand that it's just a coat. And never turn your back. And don't cycle. I saw a programme where someone mountain biking in California was attacked. If you're crouched down cycling you could look like prey. You mustn't look like prey.'

'Alex, stop worrying. I'm sure there isn't a mountain lion out here. We don't have them in Scotland. Only wild cats and domestic cats, and they won't hurt us. Although your Uncle Archie's favourite book when he was little has a story about a man being killed by a wild cat…it couldn't possibly be true though…'

'I really think we should check around before you let the hens out.'

'Ok, let's check around together.' She smiled and put her arm around his shoulders. 'Keep that brolly handy.'

She doesn't believe me, Alex thought. She thinks it was a dream and she doesn't believe me. They walked around the garden together. Nothing. Everything was as it should be. There were more raspberries, perfectly ripe and ready to pick even though they'd had bowls full the day before. Aunty Clara stopped to eat a few.

'Well,' she said, 'I'm going to let my girls out now. I don't think there's any need to worry. If it wasn't a dream, perhaps it was just a shadow you saw, made large by the moonlight. The mind can play funny tricks, especially at night.'

They could hear the chickens scrabbling inside their house, eager to get out.

'I think some light must penetrate the wood so that they know it's a new day,' said Clara. 'Chickens are very solar-powered.' The hens came bundling out of their door and down their little ladder. 'They seem happy enough,' said Clara.

But they would have been asleep, and hens are pretty stupid anyway, thought Alex. He looked around. Perhaps it was lurking, ready to pounce.

The chickens went straight to their food and began pecking. Nothing. No big cat emerged from the forest. He began to feel a bit silly.

'Shall we go and get our breakfast?' Clara asked.

'Ok,' said Alex. His voice sounded very small. It was just one tiny voice in the middle of a garden, surrounded by forest and mountains, the cold morning air, and the huge sky.

Archie was in the kitchen, stirring porridge. Katrina was up too and dressed already. She had brushed her long hair and tied it up in a ponytail high on her head. Alex thought it made her look like somebody who did gymnastics or tap-dancing, all neat and perky, or like a contestant on a really rubbish TV show.

'I like the coat,' Archie said, winking at Alex. 'Are you ready for your porridge?'

Alex slipped off his uncle's coat, it was so heavy that his shoulders seemed to float upwards as the weight left them. Aunty Clara quietly put her umbrella back in the stand.

'Is it raining out there?' Archie asked.

'No,' said Clara. She gave him a "don't ask" look.

Katrina had set the table with the blue and white stripy bowls.

'This is ready,' said Archie. He brought the pan over to the table and began to ladle out the porridge.

'I don't know if I'm very hungry,' said Alex, eyeing the cardboard-coloured gloop. It looked like part of the paper-recycling process. They'd had to watch a really boring programme about it at school.

'Ach, come on. It'll set you up for the day,' said Archie. Though he gave Alex a slightly smaller than normal portion.

'Can I get some raspberries for mine?' said Katrina, who had already taken a generous swirl of maple syrup. She pushed her chair back from the table.

'No!' shouted Alex. 'You shouldn't go out there by yourself!'

'What?'

'I saw something – like a creature – a cat – in the night. It was on the roof. It might not be safe!'

'What? said Katrina again. 'You think it's dangerous to go in the garden? Don't be stupid.'

And she went. Alex followed her to the door and then watched as she crossed the lawn. The sun was bright now and made him blink. Katrina soon returned with a handful of raspberries. 'Well, I didn't get eaten,' she said. 'Raspberry anybody?'

Alex shook his head and went back to the table.

'I really did see something,' he said. 'And so did Mr. Tom. He hissed and then hid in my bed. That's proof. It was really big and I saw the outline. It was on Aunty Clara's studio roof. I saw it.'

'I think you were dreaming,' Clara said gently. 'Dreams can be so vivid. Especially when we're away from home with stuff to worry about.'

'You said that already, but I wasn't!' said Alex. 'And I'm not hungry.' He pushed his bowl away and ran upstairs. He threw himself down on the bed. It had been there. He had seen it. Mr. Tom had seen it.

He soon heard two sets of footsteps. Why couldn't they just leave him alone?

'Alex, you don't have to have porridge if you'd rather have something else. Toast maybe, or a yoghurt. We could go into town and buy some other cereal for a change,' said Aunty Clara. His face was buried in the pillow so she stroked his bluey-black hair.

'You twins have such beautiful hair. Like ravens' wings.'

Alex shook his head, trying to dislodge her hand.

'Come on, Alex,' said Katrina. 'Nobody's laughing at you. Come back down. Uncle Archie's got to go to work soon...'

Alex heard them picking up his pencils.

'Cool books, Aunty Clara,' said Katrina.

'Oh, that *How To Draw Animals* was what really got me started. You and Alex could have a go at some of them today.'

'Come on, Alex,' said Katrina. 'I might be able to draw as well as you with this.'

He slowly sat up. They weren't laughing now, not even with their eyes.

'I was going to draw Mr. Tom last night; he came and fell asleep on my pillow. Or this tiger, look.' He found the page and showed them. 'I was just thinking about it, when Uncle Archie put the light out. You'd been asleep for hours,' he told his sister. He gave her a superior look.

'So,' said Katrina. 'You were going to draw Mr. Tom and he was asleep on your pillow, or maybe a tiger from this book, which happens to have lots of pictures of big cats, and then you fell asleep. And then you woke up because there was a big cat outside on the roof. But you Definitely Weren't Dreaming. Come on, Alex…'

'I was not dreaming,' said Alex. 'It sounds like I might have been, but I wasn't. You don't have to believe me if you don't want to. But I know what I saw.' He glared at them both, green eyes flashing anger.

'Ok, ok,' said Clara. 'Let's just agree to disagree about this. Now why don't you come down and have some breakfast? Maybe we'll go into town today. See what's on at the cinema or something. Ok?'

'Ok,' said Alex. Katrina nodded, but she gave the animals book a meaningful look and carefully propped it up on the windowsill.

Back downstairs, Archie was getting his boots on. He opened his mouth to say something, but Clara shook her head.

'Bye, love,' she said.

'I'll see you guys later,' said Archie. He gave Aunty Clara a kiss on the nose. Katrina sighed. If only, she thought, if only her mum had someone like Uncle Archie to give her a kiss on the nose when he left for work in the morning. Maybe that was what Mum needed. Archie must have heard the sigh. He gave Katrina a hug and Alex a pat on the shoulder.

'Don't forget your sandwiches,' said Aunty Clara.

Alex went to the window to watch Uncle Archie drive away, wishing that he could go with him. Maybe he'd ask if he could go with him for a day instead of hanging around with Katrina and Aunty Clara. But Uncle Archie didn't drive away. He sat in the Land Rover for a moment, and then he got out again. Alex watched as his uncle walked down to the bottom of the garden where the henhouse was and peered over the wall towards where the forest started. He stood there for a moment just looking, then he walked back towards the house. He stopped a few feet away from Aunty Clara's studio and looked up at the roof. Then he looked back towards the henhouse. Then he shrugged and went back to the van. This time he did drive away.

Alex turned from the window. So, Uncle Archie thought it was worth taking a look. Uncle Archie thought that there might have been something there.

'I quite feel like going into town,' Katrina said, spreading honey on her third bit of toast.

'Well, we'll do some shopping, get Mr. Tom a new tag for his collar, and wander about a bit. There might be a film on you'd like to see. I love going to the cinema in the afternoon,' said Aunty Clara. 'We'll have a look in the library too. Eat up.'

After some shopping and waiting for Mr. Tom's new tag to be engraved, they went to the library. Aunty Clara introduced them to one of the ladies behind the counter.

'Audrey, this is my nephew Alex and my niece Katrina, up for the holidays.'

'Pleased to meet you both,' she said. The twins made polite smiles and hoped she wouldn't ask anything else. She looked quite fierce, Katrina thought, like an osprey that might swoop down at any moment with its talons spread, an osprey with steely-grey feathers, and steel-rimmed glasses perched on its beak.

'You'll be after some holiday reading, then? Children's is over there and Young Adults is next to the computers. I'd offer you one of my chocolates, but we're not meant to eat in the library, are we, she said, pushing a box of Celebrations towards them.

Katrina smiled properly.

'I need books on cats. Big cats,' Alex said.

'School project, is it? Third aisle from the bottom on the right.'

'Thanks. How many are we allowed?'

'I've got my card and Archie's,' said Clara. 'He doesn't have anything out at the moment. You can have loads.'

Katrina went to the children's section, hoping that she wouldn't have read all the books already.

'Look, Aunty Clara, a new Sophie Anderson book. I really like her. I didn't think you'd get the latest books up here,' said Katrina.

'We are quite civilized, you know. We have books and bands and concerts and a theatre…'

Clara indicated a rack of leaflets and a huge noticeboard. Katrina spotted a poster advertising her aunt's art classes. It had a border of paint brushes and palettes.

'There might be things you'd like to do or see. Let's have a look.'

'Alex and I used to collect leaflets for things like museums and theme parks. We liked them because they were free. We've stopped now.' She pulled out some at random.

Highland Folk Museum, *A New Culloden Experience*, *Orchestra of the Highlands and Islands – Summer Tour*, *The World of Nessie*… and slipped them into Aunty Clara's bag.

There weren't any films they wanted to see. The new James Bond would be coming soon, so they thought they'd leave it until then. They had lunch in a café that overlooked the river.

'Why don't we go swimming, then?' said Clara, looking down at the churning, icy water. A duck was struggling to swim against the current. They watched as she seemed to give up and allow herself to be swept back the way she had come.

'In there?' said Alex, aghast.

'No, silly. At The Leisure Pool – Sandy McPherson told me it was wonderful. It has those slides and tunnels and jets that knock you off your feet and waterfalls that crash down on your head. But nice and warm.'

'We haven't got swimming things,' said Katrina.

'So, what?' said Clara. 'We'll go and buy some. I could do with some new towels too. Nearly ten years ago, I remember your mum saying that Archie and I had 'the towels of the newly married'. Well they're all threadbare and stringy now. Perhaps your tenth wedding anniversary should be your towelling one, not your tin foil one, or whatever it is…'

Katrina laughed. Alex looked baffled.

In the shop, Katrina and Alex tried to give Aunty Clara the money that Pippa and Brian had given them.

'Can't I buy my nephew and niece something useful? Keep it. There might be something you really want, something frivolous. That's what holiday money is meant for.'

She wouldn't let them pay for the swimming either.

'I've always wanted to come here,' she said. 'But I thought I needed some kids to come with. They might not let you in without any children.'

Soon they were entering a noisy blue world of gushes and waves and flumes. When you swim, Katrina thought, you should be able to be really alone, private and safe from everything. But it wasn't like that. A crocodile squirted her, an elephant spouted water from its trunk, and there were turquoise and yellow dolphins that you were meant to want to ride on. Katrina waded past bands of squealing toddlers and gangs of mean-looking kids half her age who were jostling to get on the motorbikes (the faster you pedalled, the further the jet of water shot from the headlamps). She saw Aunty Clara disappearing towards the big pool to swim lengths by herself. There was a notice up that said "No Children In Main Pool Until 2.30pm". Katrina had no idea where Alex had got to.

On a slightly higher level was another area with a jacuzzi. Katrina would have loved to go in that, but it was packed full of mums holding babies and laughing.

The water from the jacuzzi cascaded down into the play pool in constant sheets. You could slip behind them, like going behind a waterfall. Katrina had always wanted to go behind a waterfall. She dived under the curtain of water and suddenly she was all alone. She put one arm and then a shoulder into the cascade. The force was immense, but it was nice to be pummeled. She offered the water her other shoulder, then she turned round so that she was facing away from the pool and could see nothing but the tiled wall. She let the water fall onto her back. All other sounds were obliterated; there was only the constant crashing of the water. From the other side she would just be a blur, an anonymous figure in a blue costume, close to invisible. She was drenched, truly soaked. Water dripped from her hair and down her face, but nobody was watching her. For the first time in what seemed like a very long time, she let the tears fall. They streamed down her face. Katrina cried because everything was stupid, because her mum had smashed the mirror and abandoned them, because she had no friends for hundreds of miles, because she didn't want to go to Bleakhill Academy in the autumn, and most of all because she just wanted everything to be normal and her mum to be normal and happy.

She stayed behind her curtain of water and cried. She cried until she felt dry inside, until she had no tears left. Then she took a deep breath and ducked back under the waterfall. The "No Children" sign by the main pool was gone, so she went to swim lengths with her aunt.

Starlight. She pours herself over the wall – inhales the sweet, warm smell of feathers and eggs. She circles the wooden house of birds, nudges it, leaves scent from her muzzle. It is too heavy. There is no way in, for now.

She pads across sharp stones. This is a place of people. She smells harsh smells, measures herself against cold metal. With one bound she finds soft grass. On hind legs she stretches, extends her claws, rips through soft bark.

She knows without seeing – a tiny brother hides – she could have him – one swipe of a paw. She circles again – sweet, sweet birds – but not for her tonight. She slinks away. Her shadow is lost in the forest.

Chapter 13

It was raining, the sort of non-stop Highland mizzle that doesn't seem too bad at first, but soon proves to be all-enveloping, all-soaking. Alex sat at a spare table in Aunty Clara's studio, drawing big cats from the books he'd got from the library with the *How To Draw Animals* method. After the swimming pool they'd gone into a little shop that sold postcards and toys and things. He'd bought a pack of playing cards with pictures of Cats of The World. As well as tiger (Siberian and Bengal) and African lion and cheetah and leopard, it had the ones that lots of people hadn't heard of – Iriomote Cat, Pallas's Cat, Pampas Cat, Geoffroy's Cat, Flat-headed Cat, Fishing Cat and Marbled Cat. Alex wondered if there were more than 52 types of wild cat. The cardmakers had used Liger and Australian Marsupial Cat for the jokers so must have been struggling for ideas.

Aunty Clara was working on some watercolours of otters for the Skye Otter Trust. Katrina had spent ages practising her flute, playing *The Entertainer* again and again, until Alex had put his hands over his ears, and Aunty Clara had said that perhaps she should do something else. Now Katrina was working with some clay, but nothing would go right.

'I hate clay. Everything I do turns out terrible,' she wailed. 'I have these ideas for beautiful things, but they come out pathetic, like something I would have done at pre-school, not even as good as something Alex would have done at pre-school!'

'Don't be silly. They'll be lovely if you keep at it,' said Aunty Clara.

Katrina looked across at her aunt. She knew that Clara hadn't even looked at the sad little clay pots and figures whose legs were too thick and whose arms were too skinny and short. Katrina splatted one of the pots. She flicked the head off one of the figures. Then she screwed the rest of them into one big ball and chucked it back into the tub. Her brother and aunt carried on with their perfect pictures.

'Can I go on the computer?'

'Mmm,' said Clara, still not looking up. 'Wash your hands first.'

There was a thin layer of clay drying on Katrina's hands. It looked like mud from the Thames back home. When they'd done the Victorians in Year 5, Katrina had thought that mudlark would be by far the best of the horrible jobs done by poor children. She'd written about how it would be exciting never knowing what you'd find, coins, shells, lost jewellery, things that had fallen off ships, like beachcombing for a living. Mrs Beasley had written a bossy little note – Katrina could still remember it word for word:

Katrina, have you forgotten that the River Thames would have been a stinking place, polluted from factories and running with raw sewage? Think of the diseases! And where do you think people threw dead dogs and cats?

Katrina had written a note back:

Mrs Beasley, have you forgotten that you aren't meant to start sentences with And? And where do you think people throw teachers they hate?

But she'd crossed it out with biro hundreds of times, covering it in scribbled circles so that it was truly illegible. But knowing it was still there made her smile.

It took quite a while to wash the clay off. She loved the feeling of scrubbing her nails. Afterwards the skin felt so dry that she helped herself to a squirt of the special rose hand-cream that Aunty Clara used after she'd been gardening. It smelt lovely. She knew her aunt wouldn't notice and wouldn't mind if she did.

The study where the computer was seemed to belong to Uncle Archie. (Katrina thought this was only fair, after all Clara had her studio.) It was the darkest room in the house, and most of the books in it were his. Katrina liked reading the spines of them – *A Field Guide To The Identification of Pebbles*, *Beechcombings: the Narratives of Trees*, *Whistling in the Dark: In Pursuit of the Nightingale*, *Whales, Dolphins and Seals: A Field Guide to Marine Mammals of the World…*

There were plans for the old barn on his desk. It was going to be made into a holiday cottage. Uncle Archie had told them that the council had said 'yes' and that the builders were going to start when they'd finished another job in the village. Archie and Clara were going to rent it out to holiday people, but Katrina, Alex and their mum would sometimes be able to stay there too. She pushed the plans to one side so that she could get to the keyboard.

She switched on the computer and sat in the comfy black chair and slowly span herself around a few times. She began to remember all the things she had been trying to forget about. It was as though she and Alex had been lifted out of their normal lives and left everything – school, friends, London, and of course, Mum – behind. It was hard to imagine it all going on without them.

School would be finished by now. She was a bit sad to have missed the last few days. Those were usually fun, or they would have been for someone who didn't have Mum to worry about. One of the worst ever moments flashed into her mind: Sports Day in Year 4.

They hadn't expected Mum to come. Alex wasn't in the final of anything, and although Katrina was in the final of the 200 metres, and in the relay, Mum had said that she had a rehearsal and then lunch with some of the orchestra somewhere near Primrose Hill. But she had appeared just before Katrina's race and had cheered too loudly all the way through it, and when Katrina had come second she kept on and on saying 'But you were the best, darling, even if you didn't win. You were the best. That other girl was cheating. You were the best really, darling...' Her voice was too loud. Katrina and Alex hissed at her to stop. Everybody was looking. She didn't even shut up when Danielle Oataway went up to get her certificate. Katrina had never liked Danielle Oataway with her neat blonde plait that was always way too high up on her head, and who always had a silly extra hairtie at the top, as though she were trying to impress everybody with how many hair-ties she had. Now the dislike turned to apologetic confusion. Then Mum lay face down on the grass and fell asleep. At least it meant she shut up. Other parents had brought rugs to sit on and flasks of tea and cold drinks, and boxes with grapes and strawberries in. Mum had nothing with her but a battered old basket that was her current handbag. The contents were trying to escape onto the school field. Katrina shoved them back in – a roll of sheet music, an address book, some lipsticky tissues, her purse, which felt even lighter and emptier than usual, a little bottle of vodka that was almost empty, and the letter about the Sports Day, all screwed up. Mum's skirt was all bunched up above her knees. Katrina smoothed it down and tried to make it look as neat as possible.

Mum slept on whilst the rest of the certificates were given out. Katrina had to go up for her relay team's third prize. Mum stayed asleep. Alex lay down next to her and pretended to be having a casual little nap to try to make it all look normal. Then the sports day was over and everybody else was going home. Once all the equipment had been put away Mr. Grey, the caretaker, came over. He was holding a big bunch of keys and the twins could see that he wanted to lock the gates and get home himself. Katrina told him that Mum had just got back from a long trip with her orchestra and so she was really tired. And then Mum had woken up and there was wetness which must have been dribble all over her sleeve where her mouth had been resting, and the imprint of grass on one of her cheeks. She'd given Mr. Grey a huge mad smile and asked, 'Are you my children's teacher?'

'No, love. I'm the caretaker.'

'Oh, what a pity, I was going to ask you for a lift.'

'Came on my bike. Would you kids like to go to the office and ring your dad?'

'We'll be fine, Mr. Grey,' said Katrina.

'Yes, Mr. Caretaker,' Mum had slurred, 'We'll be fine.'

Then Mum had staggered to her feet and they'd all staggered home. Once they were back at the boat, Mum had fallen asleep again and the twins had made themselves some toast for dinner. The next day, Mum had been fine, though it was clear that she couldn't remember anything about Sports Day, or Danielle Oataway, or Mr. Grey.

Katrina had expected to be called into the school office or for somebody to ask about their mum, but nobody ever did.

The next year Katrina hadn't run her fastest in the heats so that she wouldn't qualify for any of the finals. (There was no danger of Alex ever qualifying for anything. He could often beat her when it was just the two of them, but there was something about races at school that made him stumble.) They told Mum that there was really no point in her coming, but she did anyway. This time Mum was her lovely self, brought strawberries and cherries to share, chatted to teachers and other mums, and bought ice creams on the way home. They hadn't ever talked about the year before, and Katrina knew that they never would.

The computer was ready now. Katrina hadn't been online for days. She felt so far away from it all – and what would she say to everybody? My mum went crazy and abandoned us and that's why I missed the end of term, the end of our time in Year 6? Maybe it would be easier to think up something now she was far away from everybody. Their mum had said they could have phones when they started at Bleakhill, but they hadn't even looked at any yet.

She looked at her friends' videos and photos of end of term parties. Aunty Clara had said she'd ring the school to explain that their mum was ill and that they were taking an early holiday.

'But you aren't allowed to take holidays in term-time!' Katrina had protested.

'What are they going to do, expel you? There's only a week or so to go. Don't worry. It'll be fine.' But Katrina didn't want to be the sort of person who took holidays without permission in term-time. She just wanted her life to be sensible. Well, it was too late now.

Katrina commented on one of the photos:

Sorry I missed the party. Staying with my aunty and uncle in Scotland. It's near Loch Ness but we haven't seen any monsters yet. Even Mr. Tom has come. My aunt is an artist with a really cool studio. They have 8 hens and are getting a puppy, but after we've gone home because Mr. Tom would hate it.

She didn't mention her mum.

She sat back and stared at the screen for a while. Nobody liked what she had written. Perhaps everybody had forgotten her already, or they were all at the cinema with their phones switched off, or on expensive holidays in other time zones – some of them were already on holiday in villas with their own pools and had been posting about that too. She started to scroll back through people's posts. Every so often there was an image of her. But was that really her? It seemed like some other person now, a Katrina that she had left behind in London. Would she ever be joined up with that Katrina again? The Bluebell and Mum seemed so far away. She thought of Mum in that clinic, and the boat all locked up. She hoped Pippa and Brian were looking after everything. Her friends were all going off to different schools. She wished that she was going to St. Gwendoline's like Annabella and Lulu, but there was no chance of that, Mum would never be able to afford the fees, not in a million years.

She and Alex had been for a taster day at Bleakhill. It had been ok, much as they'd expected, big and grey and noisy, with the teachers all pretending that they were going to have such a great time. Alex had hated it. Katrina knew that they'd survive, they were tough, but she didn't especially want to go there. It seemed that, as with most things in life, she wouldn't have much choice.

As she sat, staring at the screen, Annabella posted a video of herself and her big sister. They were lounging on a huge inflatable white swans in Florida. Katrina's finger hovered, ready to like it. It was one of her ambitions to go on holiday somewhere with a private pool, that and to have a bedroom that had its own bathroom. Lots of her friends had their own bathrooms, they just thought that was normal. She quite hated it when they came to tea on The Bluebell (which only happened when Katrina was 100% sure that Mum was going to be ok). They said everything was cute and really sweet, and how it must be like being on a little holiday all the time, and wondered where on earth she kept her clothes, because they would never have room to keep all of their clothes in just two drawers...

There was a knock at the front door. Katrina glanced down at the time on the computer 3.39. Too early for Uncle Archie, anyway he'd have his key. Aunty Clara wouldn't have heard it in

94

the studio. She got up, not bothering to like Annabella's video, and went to see who it was. At least she had a proper front door to open here.

The rain had stopped, and standing on the worn stone step was Sandy McPherson. Instead of the grim old man's nod he'd first greeted her with, he had a shy smile. He looked nice when he smiled, he had nice white teeth, very clean-looking and evenly spaced. He looked a bit like Ron Weasley in the *Harry Potter* films, or like the sort of boy who would be used in an ad when they wanted to have a redhead to contrast with some darker kids and a blond one.

'Hi Katrina.'

Katrina smiled back.

'Hi. Are you looking for Uncle Archie? He's not back from work yet.'

'I was kind of looking for you, you and your brother. I was wondering if you might like to, you know...'

'Ok.'

'There aren't that many kids around here, or there's not much to do, if you're used to London like you two must be. I thought you might be bored...'

Katrina had to listen, really concentrate at first, to understand everything Sandy said. She worried that she might answer a question he hadn't asked.

'We live on a boat, a houseboat. We don't go out much in London the way you might think people in London do.'

'A houseboat – that sounds cool.'

'It can be pretty freezing actually, and there isn't much space. Not like your house.'

Katrina thought of the two kitchens and the various front and back doors, his posh scary mum....

She stared past Sandy's shoulder, there were hens pecking about in the garden as usual. She realised that she was standing with the door wide open – Mr. Tom still hadn't been allowed out. 'Shall we go and find Alex? He's in my aunt's studio.'

'Ok.'

Katrina forgot about the computer and carefully closed the door behind herself. It was the sort of old-fashioned farmhouse door with a latch so that it could be closed without being locked. She led Sandy around the side of the house. Their footsteps made a lovely crunching sound in the gravel, as though they were walking on a beach.

Alex looked a bit horrified when she walked in with Sandy, so she smiled and gave him a look which said 'Don't worry – I'm quite pleased to see him – it's ok – maybe he's not so bad.'

Aunty Clara intercepted it and smiled too.

'Sandy,' she said, 'nice of you to come over. How are the puppies?'

'They're grand, thanks Mrs. Carmichael,' Sandy said, briefly turning back into the polite visitor. 'And Dad said, maybe the twins would like to borrow some of the bikes we've got in the shed. There's ones that might fit them. He says that with four boys you end up with lots of bikes.'

Alex smiled. They hadn't had bikes for ages. They'd grown out of the first proper bikes they'd had, and never got any others. Alex hoped that they wouldn't have forgotten how to do it. Boys like Sandy would never forget how to ride a bike.

'Thanks,' the twins said with one voice.

'You could come over and see the puppies and then cycle back.'

'Maybe tomorrow, then,' said Clara, looking at her watch and then back at her work. 'I don't really want to drive over now. But would you like a drink, Sandy? You must be thirsty after the ride over.'

'Yes, please, Mrs. Carmichael.'

'Clara, please. Not Mrs. Carmichael. Only the bank calls me Mrs. Carmichael. I've just come to a good place to stop for a little while,' she said, wiping the nib of the pen she'd been using, and giving a long appraising look at the picture of oyster catchers at low tide.

'Why don't you go and muck about outside, pick a few raspberries for the hens, and I'll give you a shout in a minute.'

They wandered across the grass to the henhouse. The hens looked up expectantly at the children's approach.

'Sorry, Mrs Speckledy,' said Katrina, 'We haven't got anything for you yet.'

Alex was always amazed at how Katrina could talk to animals and small children in silly or baby voices in front of people who were virtual strangers. He would have felt really stupid doing that. Katrina could do it without a second thought. Now she started to go on about the hens.

'Mrs Speckledy is one of the bosses really, one of the leaders, she's quite old, about six, I think. Aunty Clara had two at first, but Mrs Speckledy's sister died. And that one is Dolly, and that one is Dilly, they're sisters, and that one's Sally and that one, that Black Rock, is Lily. The Rhode Island Red with the funny foot is called Dorothy. She's almost as old as Mrs Speckledy. She came when Mrs Speckledy's sister died. One of Aunty Clara's friends was getting rid of her because of her foot. They thought the other hens would pick on her, so Aunty Clara took her in.'

'Not many folks would've kept her,' said Sandy, suddenly looking thirty years older, giving the twins a glimpse of the farmer he would be.

They all looked down at Dorothy's feet. With all hens you only have to look at their legs and claws to see that they are dinosaurs' closest living relatives. The toes on Dorothy's left foot weren't spread out properly though, and the claws sort of curled over to the side.

'But she's been fine. Aunty Clara has to clip her claws sometimes. I helped her last time. I'm going to be a vet.'

Sandy smiled at her.

'In London, just with city pets, or up here?' he asked.

'I don't know yet. I like countryside. I wouldn't want to do all spoilt little dogs, you know, Chihuahuas. And I hate those Mexican hairless dogs. This girl at school even had a hairless cat. It was some really rare American breed and cost eight hundred pounds, and I thought it would be awful when I heard about it, but it was really silky and warm. But I like farm animals. I just need to learn a bit more. I'm good at chickens already.'

As if to prove this, Katrina confidently picked up one of the Black Rocks. She tucked her arm around it so that it would feel reassured and wouldn't flap and offered it to Sandy and Alex to stroke. The feathers were soft and warm and smooth and shiny.

'This one is Ruby, and that other Black Rock is Gertie,' she said. 'My mum thinks Aunty Clara called her Gertie because she'd started to worry that she'd have used up all of the nice girls' names before she ever had a baby. You'd never want to call a baby "Gertie", would you? Or "Mrs Speckledy". There are lots of girls called Lily and Ruby and a few Dorothies at school…' She sensed that Sandy might not be very interested in girls' names. 'Let's get some raspberries,' she said.

'We've got hens. A few hundred of them,' said Sandy.

'Oh,' said Katrina. 'Then you'd know what they like.'

'We don't really bother doing things like giving them raspberries. It's too busy on the farm. They just have their layers' pellets and scratch feed and scraps sometimes and get on with it. They aren't really pets like your Aunty's.'

'Oh, these are hard-workers too,' said Katrina, sticking her chin out. 'Look.' She opened up one of the egg collection doors at the side of the house – four pale brown eggs were there.

Alex turned his back on them. It was typical of Katrina to try and be the expert on hens to someone who had hundreds of them and owned half of Scotland. He wandered over to the brambles in one of the corners of the garden to see if any of the blackberries were ripe yet. The ancient stone wall was low, and it seemed that the undergrowth from the forest was about to encroach on the garden, ready to reabsorb it into the wild if the humans looked away for a few days too long. Was there a big cat out there? He looked and looked. Nothing.

Some of the blackberries looked ripe. The first one was gorgeous, sweet and juicy. But after that they all seemed to be sour and bitter. He picked a handful anyway and walked back towards the others and the hens. He loved the way the hens all went around together in a friendly group. They seemed to be interested in things and places at the same time, and when one decided she wanted a dustbath, the others would all soon think it was a good idea too. He remembered being little, he must have been around four or five, and spotting a hen on her side on the ground with one wing extended and flapping. He'd run in shouting, 'Aunty Clara! Quick! One of your hens is dying!' She had come running, only to stop and laugh.

'That's how they take a bath, Alex, a dust bath. They love it. It must get all of the grime and any little insects out of their feathers.'

He knew much more about hen behaviour now, but he wouldn't have boasted about it the way Katrina did. The hens came running for the blackberries, and then he picked them a few raspberries. Sandy and Katrina came to join him and they stood there in friendly silence, eating raspberries and throwing them for the hens. Soon the children's lips were stained pinky-purple with berry juice. Sandy's lips were the pinkest, but they had a head-start, being a slightly ridiculous bright colour to begin with. Alex was glad that he didn't have lips like that. School was hard enough without having bright red lips. His own mouth was wide, the lips were thin and quite pale, exactly the same as his dad's in the photos they had.

And Sandy, Alex thought, *was* a bit of a silly name, or it would be in London. But he couldn't imagine anyone teasing Sandy. There was something tough about Sandy, despite the lips. He looked like he'd be good at all sports. He probably always wore that Inverness C.T. football shirt, although Alex could imagine him in a Scottish rugby shirt. The McPhersons looked like they'd be big rugby fans.

They wandered over to the tyre swing.

'You can have first go,' Katrina told Sandy.

'Thanks.'

Sandy climbed into the tyre and was soon swinging high. Katrina looked on enviously. It was amazing how much and how quickly you could envy the person who was on the only swing when you were waiting for your turn. She was just about to say something when Aunty Clara appeared at the back door

'Twins – your mum's on the phone!'

Sandy was left, forgotten and swinging. Katrina and Alex sprinted, got there at almost the same moment, and reached for the phone with identical gestures. Alex dropped his arm and let Katrina go first; suddenly he couldn't think of much to say anyway.

'Hi Mum,' Katrina panted.

'Hi Honey. Are you ok?'

'We're fine, Mum. It's great here…' Katrina immediately regretted saying that. What should she say? She was really missing her mum. She didn't want to sound *too* happy, but she did want to sound ok. What did you say to your mum who was hundreds of miles away in some stupid clinic?

'Are you ok, Mum?'

'I'm much better. It's so good to hear your voice. Sweetheart, I'm so sorry about all of this. I didn't mean this to happen. I'm so relieved you're with Clara and Archie. Is Mr. Tom ok?'

'He's fine.' Katrina had a picture of Mr. Tom and the broken mirror, then having to go out to get food for him, and then the man in the shop saying "Your mum very bad".

'Um, they're going to get a new puppy, but it's not ready yet,' she said.

'I'm really missing you, you know,' Mum said.

'We're really missing you too.' Then Katrina couldn't think of anything else to say. 'Alex wants to talk to you,' she said. 'He's right here.'

'I love you, Katrina.'

'You too, Mum. Here's Alex'.

Katrina handed the phone to her brother, and stood there whilst he had an almost identical conversation. He soon handed the phone back to Aunty Clara who wandered back to the kitchen with it.

The twins walked slowly back towards the tree with the swing. Sandy was in the hammock now, and was rocking himself to and fro.

'You have to be careful,' Katrina told him. 'It's very old and it might break at any moment.'

'I'm ok,' Sandy said. Alex noticed him give Katrina a look. He obviously thought that she could be a bit bossy. Well, he wasn't alone there.

'Hey!' Katrina suddenly barked. 'Why did you do that to our tree?' There were long gashes on the trunk, half-obliterating the initials that the twins had carved on their first afternoon. The boys followed her gaze. Sandy tipped himself out of the hammock to have a closer look.

'Uh? What do you mean? I haven't done anything to your tree – you're the ones who've damaged it – trees can die if you remove too much bark,' said Sandy.

'We didn't do all that – we only did tiny initials when we were bored,' Alex joined in.

'Well I didn't do it either. I don't go round damaging trees. Farmers don't do things like that.'

There were long wounds in the bark. They started about a foot above where the twins had put their initials. Alex and Katrina had been careful not to carve too deeply; these gashes ripped into the bark and went right down the trunk, ending a bit higher than the twins' knee-level.

'I didn't do that,' said Sandy. 'How would I? I haven't got anything on me! And I didn't do it with my fingernails, did I?'

He spread his fingers, which were rather stumpy, although his hands were large and thick and square. His nails were almost painfully short. It looked either as though he bit them or as if someone mean and strict cut them for him.

'Well someone did it,' said Katrina. 'And it wasn't us, and it wouldn't exactly have been Aunty Clara or Uncle Archie, would it?'

'I don't think somebody could have done it whilst they were in the hammock, done it with their feet and not noticed,' said Alex. They stared at the scratches and one by one put their fingers in them.

'They're really weird, aren't they,' said Katrina.

'You know,' said Sandy. 'They are just like the wounds on that heifer of ours. Those were deep, and about this far apart. They went right down its rump.'

'It's horrible having our initials scratched out. But who could have done it?' Katrina wondered out loud. 'I think it was either some mad person, but that doesn't seem very likely, or a creature did this.'

'I told you,' said Alex. 'I saw a big cat in the garden, in the night. You didn't believe me, Katrina, but I did. I wasn't dreaming. Mr. Tom saw it too. It was here.'

They all looked long and hard at the marks on the tree.

'These are claw-marks,' said Alex. 'There's a creature, and I've seen it.'

Chapter 14

They heard Uncle Archie's Land Rover approaching before they saw it. Aunty Clara came out to meet him. The three children watched as he kissed her on the cheek and she hugged him. He sat on the bench by the door to take his boots off.

'Tea!' Aunty Clara shouted.

'Shall we tell them what we think?' Katrina asked.

'They'd think we were just kids playing a game. I know my Dad'd think it was rubbish.' said Sandy.

'There are the scratches, and what happened to your heifer...' said Katrina.

'And what I saw the other night,' said Alex. 'Clara thought it was a dream, but I think Uncle Archie might have believed me. I saw him having a look.'

'And when I went out with Ed the vet, something had really frightened this little dog, but the owner didn't see anything.'

'You went on a visit with Ed Stirling?' asked Sandy, impressed. Katrina nodded.

'I helped him do loads of stuff.'

'Cool,' said Sandy. 'But, let's think about it, before we say anything to the grown-ups. It could be anything. There's any number of explanations.' Sandy knew what it was like to be the youngest child, the one whose ideas were dismissed as silly, the one who people treated as a baby. And he really liked the Carmichaels. He didn't want them to think he was stupid.

'Tea!' Aunty Clara called again, across the garden.

'We won't say anything, then,' said Alex. Katrina and Sandy nodded and they followed him indoors.

'I think we could let Mr. Tom out now, don't you?' Aunty Clara said, passing a plate of scones towards Alex.

He took one and then helped himself to the jam, which was raspberry and home-made. He didn't like cream or butter much. Katrina did. She liked anything that was creamy or cheesy or milky or chocolaty. Did identical twins like the same foods? He didn't know. Katrina liked macaroni cheese. It was one of his most hated foods. He liked things that were really sour or lemony or pickled. But they both liked scones and jam and cake, but then didn't everybody?

'What do you think twins, shall we let him out? He must be getting bored. He's got this address on his tag now, but I don't think he'd get lost. It's up to you though, you know him best.'

'Maybe,' said Katrina. 'Maybe in a few days…'

'Yeah,' said Alex. 'I don't know if he's ready for it yet. We wouldn't want him to go missing or anything…'

'Ok. But he was scratching at the back door. I think he's nearly ready.'

The twins bit their lips – identical gestures – and didn't answer.

'How are the pups, Sandy? How's mine doing?' Archie asked.

'They're all grand, Mr. Carmichael. Your one's doing great. Alex and Katrina are going to come and see them tomorrow.'

'Sandy's dad said they had some old bikes that would be about the right size for us,' said Katrina.

'And we want to see the puppies and how that heifer's doing,' said Alex.

'How is it doing?' asked Archie.

'It's going to be fine. It had a shot of antibiotics so it didn't get infected. They're quite deep wounds, but it'll be back in the fields soon.'

Archie smiled and nodded. His mouth was too full of scone to say anything for a moment. He took a big swig of tea.

'I passed Ed Stirling again today,' Archie said, turning towards his wife. 'Said I'd go for a pint. Wondered if you might like to bring the twins and we could have supper in the pub...'

'Ok. Great. I'll just do a bit more work before this evening...'

'I'd better be going soon then, Mrs. Carmichael,' said Sandy when he'd finished his second scone.

'It's Clara, please,' she smiled.

'Shall we come over tomorrow morning?' Katrina asked.

'Aye. That'll be fine.'

'Thanks Mrs. Car...Clara' said Sandy, heading for the door. Mr. Tom appeared and looked as though he might follow.

'No you don't,' said Katrina, scooping him up. 'Not for a little while yet.'

'You get back to work, love,' Archie said. 'The twins and I can clear this lot up.' Clara smiled, finished her tea, and hurried away to her studio. Katrina watched her go.

'I hope you don't mind, having us here,' she said. 'I mean it is extra work for you both and we do distract Clara from painting.'

'You're no bother.' Archie got up and ruffled his niece's hair. 'You're not much of a distraction, and you're the best, the nicest distraction an aunty or uncle could have.'

'Maybe we could come to work with you one day, distract you instead…'said Alex.

'Sure,' said Archie. Clara had already disappeared.

A couple of hours later they set out in Aunty Clara's old yellow Renault. Archie always looked a bit too big to fold himself into the passenger seat. The pub was in the village, down by the loch. If you looked at a map it didn't seem far, but the roads were so twisty and turny that it took longer than you would expect.

The pub garden overlooked the loch and was popular with tourists as well as locals; they were lucky to find a table free. It was one of those picnic tables that you have to put your legs under. Archie looked too big for that too.

'Ed's always late,' he said. 'He's always got one more call to do – dedication, eh?' Katrina and Alex were well into their second J2Os by the time he arrived and had studied the menu and decided exactly what they wanted to eat. Finally Ed appeared, and Archie bought him a pint.

'Busy day?' Clara said.

'Aye, but it usually is.' Ed looked about before continuing. 'You have some animals on your books that you wish you hadn't, some owners really. There's a certain wee Westie and her owner who take up a lot of my time. Katrina and I saw them yesterday, but I had to go back again today.'

'I think I know who you mean,' said Clara, who knew everybody in the village. She smiled, and Ed rolled his eyes.

'This week there's nothing physically wrong with the beast. But she's had some sort of a fright and she won't go out. Her owner's worried. I say give it a few more days…'

'What do you think frightened her?' said Alex.

'Oh, I don't know, probably some tourist's dog. I thought it might even be an otter as it happened down by the loch and there was nobody else about. Maybe she surprised a female who had cubs to protect. They can be really fierce.'

'Do you know where exactly?' Clara asked.

'It was just down there, along where those rocks are. But don't get excited. It was probably just another dog. There are always a few tourist dogs around in the summer, causing trouble, though it does take a bit to frighten Minnie. Ah, I've told you who it was now, so much for patient confidentiality, eh? Anyway, shall we order some food?'

Katrina saw that she and Alex had accidentally finished their J2Os again. Aunty Clara was still on her first diet coke.

'We'll just have water, next time, won't we Alex?' she said.

'Katrina, you have whatever you like to drink, J2O, Scottish tap water…' Archie smiled at her. 'If I can't buy my nephew and niece a few bottles of J2O, what's the point in going to work?'

'Just water, please, Uncle Archie, or I'll be too full to eat.'

'Me too,' said Alex, though he wouldn't have minded another bottle of the apple and mango one.

It was vegetable lasagne (served with chips) for Katrina and Alex, and vegetable lasagne (served with a side salad) for Clara (who was a vegetarian too) and steak and chips (with the vegetables of the day, which were always peas and carrots, according to Archie) for the men.

Afterwards Clara said, 'Why don't we go for a stroll, twins? We could go down and look at the loch. Maybe we'll see that otter.'

They left Archie and Ed behind and went down to the water's edge. The sun was beginning to go down, the wind had dropped and the water looked inky and mysterious.

'Do you always just drink diet coke?' Katrina asked her aunt.

'Usually. Sometimes I have a glass of wine, or white wine and soda. That's nice, with lots of ice. If you don't drink very often, a little will really affect you. I find if I have more than a glass or maybe two, I'll feel awful the next day; it mucks up my head and my work. It's just not worth it.'

'I wish Mum thought that,' said Alex.

'I think it's a real poison to her,' said Clara. 'She should probably never drink again. It's just really bad for some people, as though they are allergic, and she's one of them. But nobody can make her. She's got to decide for herself. Maybe this will be the time that she does. I had a long chat with her. It sounds as though they're really doing her some good in that clinic. Her thinking seemed much clearer. I know she's really sorry about what happened.'

'Yeah, well. It has happened, and there's no point being sorry unless you're going to change, is there?' said Katrina, her mouth a hard, little line. She bent and picked up a stone and threw it as hard and as far as she could out into the loch.

110

'You've every right to be angry,' said Clara. 'The way she left you like that was, well…'

Alex bent and picked up a stone now. His went just as far as Katrina's, echoing the arc through the air exactly, and sending another circle of ripples to combine with hers.

'Sometimes,' Katrina said, 'I wish you were our mum and she was the aunty. I shouldn't have said that.'

'You say whatever you like,' said Clara. 'Sometimes I wish I were your mum, and she were your aunty too. But it is hard for her. It's hard being a musician, with all the pressure to perform.'

'But not all musicians are like Mum.'

'No. And drinking certainly won't make you into a better musician. It's only going to hold you back in the long run. Our father, your grandfather, he was an alcoholic really. Nobody ever said it at the time, but that's what he was. Some people are better at covering it up than others. He didn't go off and get lost, but he got very drunk a lot of the time. He could be very manipulative and a bit of a bully. We were lucky when we were your age, we had our mum. But she died when I was 16, and your mum was about to go to music college. It was tough for us all. I left home as soon as I could too. I loved the time I had at art school, and then of course I met Archie.'

'Mmm.' Katrina slipped her hand into her aunt's. It was sad thinking about it all, about her mum and Aunty Clara being without their own mum.

'I don't remember Grandad,' said Alex.

'Well, he died when you were both really small. He'd stopped drinking by then so he was nicer. He was really happy to have met you both.'

'So if he was an alcoholic, and then mum, will we have to be alcoholics?' Katrina asked.

'Of course not!'

Katrina gave her aunt a long hard look, but the dusk was gathering, and she suspected that Clara didn't know all the answers. By now they'd come to a place where the shingle and sand ended a mass of boulders. A stream ran down from the hills and between the boulders into the loch.

'This must be where that dog was frightened, where there was an otter or something,' said Alex. They turned around and leant against the rocks.

'Even when Mum's ok, I feel like all the trouble might just be lurking,' said Katrina. 'It seems to lurk there for Mum and then suddenly get her. What if it's lurking for us?'

'You'll know how to face it, if it's even there,' said Clara. 'You mustn't worry about it. You are both going to be fine. You're kind and clever and you've got each other and you've got me and Archie and you'll have your mum back again. She will get better. This might be the time when she realises. I know what you're like. You're both insightful and good at being happy.'

'I hate it,' said Katrina. 'It's like a shadow over us all the time. I don't really want to go back to London and be just with mum. She's missed the tour with the orchestra. I don't know if her place with them has gone now.'

'Don't worry about that now. It's not either of your job to worry about that. Archie and I will look after you.'

'We'll have to go to school sometime. We didn't finish Year 6 properly, and we haven't got any of the stuff for Bleakhill.'

'I don't want to go there anyway,' said Alex. 'Maybe we could just give up school.'

'Stop worrying. You don't have to worry about school now. It's a long time until September.'

'When you said mum was an alcoholic,' said Alex, 'well, I hadn't really thought that before. I thought alcoholics were more men and homeless. I always thought it was more sadness with mum, just a sort of terrible sadness, maybe because she has to look after us and our dad isn't there.'

'You are the biggest joy, the biggest source of happiness she has. I know. It's obvious and she's told me. She was like this before she had you. Lots of people drink too much when they're students. She did. I remember going to parties with her when she was at the Guildhall College and I was a sixth former, planning to go to art school. Most people stop after those student days. She didn't. But she will. I'm sure she will.'

'Let's go back,' said Katrina. 'I think it's a bit spooky here.'

The sky was turning the peculiar greenish colour that comes before dark, and the boulders they were leaning on felt cold and uncomfortable. They started heading back towards the village and the pub.

'I'm pleased we had this talk. Not talking about troubles, about the sadnesses and worries and shadowy things is where the trouble starts,' said Clara.

'Ok,' said Katrina.

Clara looked over at Alex, but his face was as cold and smooth as a pebble.

When they got home it was really getting dark.

'I'll do the hens,' Archie said.

'Check they're all there!' Alex called after him.

'Aye, I will.' He took the torch from where it hung by the back door.

'I'll come with you,' said Alex.

'No, you go and get your pyjamas on. I expect Clara'll be making hot chocolate.'

'I'm coming,' Alex insisted. He hurried after his uncle. They didn't need the torch to see their way across the garden.

'Check they're all in before you lock it,' said Alex.

'Ok, ok.'

Archie lifted the panel at the side and shone the torch inside. There were the hens, all lined up and snuggled together on the roosting bars.

'I'm counting them,' said Alex. 'Ok. Eight. They're all there.'

'Thanks. Am I allowed to lock it now?'

'Yes.'

With deliberate movements Archie put the panel back and locked the hens' door, then he switched off the torch and they walked back towards the house. Suddenly Alex felt something soft brush against his leg. He jumped, let out a little cry.

'Mr. Tom! What are you doing out here! How did you get out?' He picked Mr. Tom up and carried him back in.

'I think that means it's ok to let him out, don't you? I wonder how he got out.' They looked up at the house. The bathroom window was open.

'He must have got out that way, and come down over the porch,' said Archie.

'Maybe he was guarding the hens,' said Alex. 'He's a really brave cat.'

'Aye, really brave and really tough,' said Archie, ruffling his nephew's hair.

Dawn. The mist is rising. She can keep beneath it. She follows the line of stones, keeps to the edges. Here are sheep. She drops down, slinks forwards. Chooses. That one is young and tender, but small and quick. That one would be slower. She waits – empty belly low – muscles tense – her tail gives a tiny twitch, a tiny thud. Enough to betray her?

She leaps. The slow one is beneath her – woolly whiteness as tough and springy as heather – a rip, a bite – there is no struggle.

Thick, salt-sweet redness flows into her. Teeth rip, tongue rasps – work and feast, work and feast.

The others scatter and bleat. She has no need of them now. Let them cry. They can do nothing but keep their distance.

The bark of a dog, enemy dog, and she must leave. Her shadow becomes one with the trees.

Chapter 15

The black Alsatian ran out to greet them at Sandy's house, but there was no other sign of life. Aunty Clara, who had driven the twins over, made no move to get out of the car.

'So, you'll be ok to cycle back – you can see the way – just back down the road and turn right at the t-junction. But ring me if it doesn't work out with the bikes, and I'll come and get you.' Katrina was sitting in the front. Clara leant over and gave her a peck on the cheek. Then she turned and patted Alex's leg. 'Alright then?' Alex gave her a half smile. He could tell that she was desperate to get back to her studio. She had the same sort of jumpiness that Mum had when her practicing was interrupted.

'Actually, Aunty Clara, can you come for a minute. We don't want to go to the wrong door or something,' said Katrina.

Clara looked up at the house (square, solid, imposing). She thought about Mrs. McPherson (tall, thin, imposing).

'Ok, I see what you mean. And I'd like to meet the new puppy.' Sandy appeared and calmed the barking dog. He led them round the side and took them in to see the puppies.

'Oh, she's adorable! They all are,' said Clara. The puppies had reached that big-pawed, clumsy, shambling about and into everything stage. Aunty Clara knelt down and gathered her new family member into her arms. Katrina nudged Alex and grinned. Clara had tears in her eyes.

Mrs. McPherson came in.

'Clara! Lovely to see you, and the twins. Sandy's been really looking forward to having people of his own age to play with.' Sandy blushed a deep shade of strawberry – people to play with – as though he were a toddler!

'I wouldn't kneel down there if I were you, Clara, you know puppies…' Mrs McPherson bossed on.

'Oh, these are just my painting clothes,' Clara said, but she still got up as though she'd been told off.

'The twins are very welcome to stay to lunch.'

'Oh, thank you. I'm afraid they are vegetarian.'

'Vegetarian! Well, I dare say I'll find something. Do they eat chicken?'

'Er, no,' said Clara. Katrina and Alex carried on playing with the puppies, and pretended that they couldn't hear themselves being discussed.

'Cheese sandwich, anything's fine, don't go to any trouble…' said Clara.

'Oh, I won't.'

'Well, thank you, and thank you for showing me the puppies, Sandy. They couldn't be cuter.'

Mrs. McPherson disappeared with Clara.

'What do you want to do?' Sandy asked.

'Could we see round the farm?' Alex asked. 'And visit that heifer with the scratches?'

'Sure,' said Sandy. 'My Dad doesn't like visitors wandering about, but it's ok if you're with me.'

They went back out through the side door and Sandy led them off behind the house and through a large metal gate. The black Alsatian now accompanied them, trotting at Sandy's side and letting them pat it. Its name was Jet.

'What's in there?' Katrina asked, indicating the first huge barn that they came to.

'Tractors,' said Sandy. 'And a few thousand tons of potatoes. We're a mixed farm. She's in here,' he said, indicating the next barn. 'She'll be back out with the others again soon.'

The heifer was in a penned off section of the barn. She looked up when they went in and made a soft blowing sound. Katrina was about to do it back, but she stopped herself. Was that a friendly noise?

Sandy dipped his hand into a bucket of pellety things and offered some to the patient.

'You can give her some too if you like.'

'Has she got a name?' Katrina asked, letting the heifer take the food from her hand. She realised what the answer would be before it came.

'There's too many to give 'em names.'

The heifer's tongue was huge and curling, a liquorice fringe hung down between her eyes which were like liquid chocolate. Sandy patted her, quite hard, on the side of her neck, and then chucked another handful of the pellets towards the back of the stall. The heifer turned to get them and the twins could see the marks on her rump. They were healing now, but the long deep gashes had cut through the thick hide. There were four clearly visible lines on each side, thickest and deepest at the top, extending downwards by about the length of a school ruler.

'Nasty,' said Alex.

'Ugh,' said Katrina.

'Still want to be a vet?' Sandy asked her.

'Yup. I'm not squeamish – I can cope with things.'

'She can,' said Alex, remembering Katrina scooping up Mr. Tom to save his paws from the broken mirror, and being the one to start sweeping and wiping up.

'They do look like the marks on your tree, don't they?' said Sandy. The twins nodded.

'I saw something,' said Alex. 'I really did. It had the shape of a cat.'

'What about a Scottish wild cat?' said Katrina, brushing a fly away from her own fringe, which like the heifer's, could have done with a trim.

'They don't attack cattle. Much too small,' said Sandy.

'They're just like domestic cats, like big tabbies, wild, but really shy. They couldn't do this,' said Alex.

'Maybe it was some barbed wire, or machinery that she rolled on, or got caught on…' said Katrina.

'The vet said that,' said Sandy, 'but there was nothing in the field.'

'A dog?'

'Dogs don't have sharp enough claws. Their attack is their bite, isn't it?' said Alex. They all stared at the heifer who had turned round again now, hoping for more cow-nuts. Sandy gave her some.

'Let's google "scratch marks",' said Sandy. He led them back to the farmhouse and then in through the back, back door. They took off their trainers and put them in the spaces in the line of posh wellies whose owners must have been out at work somewhere on the farm. Katrina wondered if she'd ever be someone who had wellies like that. She liked Aunty Clara's better, they were pink and blue spotty. If you were a vet in the countryside you would probably have to have green wellies. They could hear Radio Four playing in the kitchen, some droning show about mortgages or something.

'Wash your hands,' said Sandy, nodding towards a little cloakroom. Then he led them up a narrow staircase (which Katrina suspected were the back, back stairs, or even the back, back, back stairs) and then along a pristine corridor. The creamy walls were exactly the same shade as the carpet.

'I can see why we took our shoes off,' said Katrina. 'And washed our hands.' She could imagine how scary Mrs. McPherson would be if there were muddy footprints or fingerprints. Sandy's bedroom was at the back of the house.

'Hey! You can see our house!' said Katrina.

'Not really our house,' said Alex. 'Our house is a houseboat.'

'You know what I mean,' Katrina snapped back, although part of her wished it *was* their house.

In the middle distance you could see the Carmichaels' house, with Clara's studio and the old barn, and beyond that the forest

120

and the haze of the Highlands in the distance. Now Katrina understood why Sandy thought he had the right to sit on her aunt and uncle's gate. If you could see it all from your bedroom window, you'd feel like it kind of belonged to you. She stepped back from the window and looked around Sandy's bedroom. It was really empty and neat, not like any kid's bedroom she'd ever seen before. In London, her friend's bedrooms were full of stuff, boxes and boxes of stuff, some of them had drawers so full of stuff that you could hardly open them. Boys were different, but were their rooms usually this plain and tidy?

The walls and carpet were exactly the same as in the hallways. Sandy had a poster of Inverness CT up above his bed. There was a pin-board in the shape of a football, but there wasn't anything pinned on it. He had a bookcase that had nothing much in apart from some school books, some football magazines in a neat pile, and a stack of computer games. His bed had a blue and white patchwork cover, the sort of thing that tried to look home-made, but wasn't. The computer on Sandy's desk looked newer than Uncle Archie's or the ones they had at school, and loads better than the one they had at home.

'Your room is so neat,' said Katrina.

'My mum's mad against mess,' said Sandy. 'She's always going on about "clutter".'

'Our mum too, though she's actually messier than we are,' said Katrina. 'But we haven't got any room on the boat. I wish I had a room this big.' Katrina imagined being able to spread her stuff out, to keep silly things.

Sandy switched the computer on – it worked really fast. He typed "scratch marks" into Google and the three of them stared at the results. There was nothing that looked as though it might be of any use, unless you had a leather sofa, or a camera with problem scratches on the lens, or some sort of bizarre medical condition.

'Try "attacks on cattle Scotland",' said Alex.

Again, nothing that looked relevant.

'Try "cat attacks Scotland",' said Alex. All that came up seemed to be about people attacking cats.

'I don't want to look at any of those,' said Katrina.

'Try "big cats Scotland",' said Alex.

'That would be saying it was a big cat,' said Katrina. 'We should be investigating everything.'

'Well I saw a big cat, or at least a cat that was very big, and this is Scotland,' said Alex.

Sandy typed in "big cats Scotland".

'Whoa,' said Katrina. 'Look at all of those – millions of results.' There were lots of articles from newspapers and on the BBC website. They read a few of those and then Sandy clicked on another one – an organization that collected sightings across the whole of the UK. Katrina and Alex knelt on the floor beside him and the three of them read in silence.

'Now try another one – go to the Scottish bit,' said Alex after a while. On they read – there were hundreds of sightings, plus paw prints found, sheep killed, lambs taken, and some of the reports were from nearby.

'Look at that one!' said Katrina.

Report from an Eyewitness in Fife

I was walking along the lane with my Jack Russell, Rascal. He's a tough little fellow, not afraid of anything. Suddenly he started whining and refused to go any further. Well I told him off, but he just wouldn't budge. So I scooped him up, ready to carry him. Then this big black cat – I was sure it was a cat – it had a cat's face and a long snakey tail – not like a dog's tail – it just leapt out in front of us. It snarled – I froze – I was too frightened to scream. Then it gave us an insolent look. It had these really piercing greeny-yellow eyes. Then it just bounded away. It leapt over the hedge – and that's at least five foot high – but it cleared it easily. I hurried up the lane to where there's a gate that you can see over, and I watched it disappear across the field and into the wood. We went straight home. I phoned the police. They said they'd had another report of a black cat near there the week before, but they didn't seem to be about to do anything. I mentioned it to my friend, and he says that his mum found these long deep scratch marks on a tree in her back garden. I won't be going down that lane for a while. I've lived in the countryside all my life, but I've never seen anything like that before.

'And that one!' said Alex.

Eyewitness report from Aberdeenshire

I'd always thought that people who say they've seen these big cats have just had one too many, but I know what I saw last night, and I hadn't been drinking. I'm a casualty nurse. It was late when I got home, well after midnight, but some impulse made me stay in the car for a minute when I pulled up in the drive. Then I caught sight of this creature. I could see it quite clearly in the headlights. It was sitting on the wall by the side of the house. It had a sandy, spotty coat and tufty ears. It looked really ugly. I couldn't believe what I was seeing. It wasn't like any dog, though I'd say it was about the size of an Alsatian. I've seen my neighbours' cat sit in just that spot –

123

and this creature was loads bigger than that. I sat there for a minute, and then beeped the horn. I was wondering if it was real. It ran off and I saw that it didn't have a proper tail. I wish I'd got a picture of it, but my phone was in my bag on the back seat. It was all just really weird.

I felt quite shaken. I went in the house and looked at pictures on the internet. It was a lynx. I'm sure of that.

'Lynxes aren't ugly!' said Katrina. 'How could anyone say a lynx was ugly? I bet she's really ugly.'

On they read.

Eyewitness Report From Perthshire

I'd noticed a big drop in the number of rabbits I see on my morning walks. I was in the field behind the caravan site where I always used to see lots of them, when I spotted this sandy-coloured thing slinking along by the hedge, close to all the rabbit warrens. At first I thought it was a Labrador. It was about that size and colour. But it didn't move like a Labrador, it was slinking and stalking like a cat. I stood still, and watched and I saw it pounce and take a rabbit. That gave me a clear idea of how big it was – this was no pet moggy. Once it had its prey it seemed to notice me. It gave me a long stare, then it bounded off with the rabbit in its mouth. I saw it had a long heavy tail, carried low, not like a dog's tail or a pet cat's tail at all.

It looked to me like a small lioness, but then I looked in one of my grandson's books, and I think it might have been a puma. It was the right colour and size for that.

'Most of them seem to be black cats, pumas or lynxes,' said Alex. 'I hope it's a lynx. I love lynxes and they belong here. I don't remember if the thing I saw had tufted ears, it was too dark, and I didn't see a tail, just its outline. I wish I'd seen if it had a tail.'

'I'm going to look on Wikipedia now,' said Sandy.

'Our teacher says Wikipedia is just for lazy people,' said Katrina, whose hand was aching to take control of the mouse.

'Aye,' said Sandy, 'but it's good for telling you stuff you need to know.'

They read in silence.

'Let's write down important bits, or can you print that out?' said Katrina, seeing that Sandy had his own printer. She didn't want to admit that the Wikipedia entry seemed useful. 'It does say it has "multiple issues", but still…'

'I'll print it,' said Sandy.

'I think you should tell your dad what you think attacked the heifer,' said Alex. 'It might strike again.'

'Maybe.'

'Do you think he'd shoot it if he saw it?' Katrina asked.

'Any farmer is going to shoot anything that attacks his livestock,' said Sandy.

'Well maybe you should just ask him what he thinks then,' said Alex.

'Ok.'

'Let's look at some more of the sightings from around here,' said Katrina. 'Have you seen that puma in the museum in Inverness? I remember seeing that when we came another time. I didn't know it actually lived here. I thought it was just a sad old stuffed puma.'

'You see that puma on every school trip. Hardly anyone even looks at it now,' said Sandy.

'Poor old thing,' said Katrina. 'Imagine ending up there, and then nobody bothers to look at you.'

A sharp voice called up the stairs:

'Sandy, lunchtime! Come and set the table.'

He shut down the computer.

'Do you want this?' he offered the twins the list from Wikipedia.

'I know what to do with it,' said Katrina. She took the article and pinned it up on Sandy's noticeboard.

'Come on, maybe we'll ask my dad what he thinks,' said Sandy, smiling. Katrina and Alex followed him, hoping that it wouldn't be chicken or fish. It was amazing how people thought vegetarians might eat chicken or fish, as if though those creatures weren't alive. Sandy led them to the kitchen where they'd first seen Mrs. McPherson bashing the steaks. This time she was shaving slices of cheese from a huge block.

'How many for?' asked Sandy.

'Just us, Bruce and your Dad. Ian and Bill are taking the Massey over to the MacDonald's.'

Alex guessed that Bruce was the third youngest of the brothers and wondered if he'd be the friendliest.

'And have you taken a look at the bikes yet?' Mrs. McPherson asked, passing Katrina a bowl of tomatoes to put on the table.

'Oh, no, not yet,' said Katrina. She realised that sounded ungrateful. 'We were looking at the puppies, and then the heifer, and then at Sandy's room. But thank you, it's really kind of you.'

Mrs. McPherson flashed Katrina a smile. Then Mr. McPherson came in, looking less like an angry giant this time,

Bruce followed him, wearing an identical red tartan workshirt. He nodded at the twins.

Please don't let her say that we are vegetarians, Katrina prayed. She could imagine how a farmer would take that, knew there would be the usual question about Christmas dinner.

'There's pie, for those that want it,' said Mrs. McPherson, 'Steak and kidney. Or cheese sandwiches for those that don't.'

'I'm happy with sandwiches, thanks,' said Sandy, smiling at Katrina.

'Me too,' said the twins, with one voice.

'Dad,' said Sandy, once everybody had started, 'what do you think did that to the heifer?' Mr. McPherson chewed and swallowed a large mouthful of pie.

'I don't know.' He took another forkful.

'It must have been something, Dad.'

'Aye, it must.'

'It couldn't have been a dog, could it?'

'Scratches that long and deep, I don't think so.'

'So, what do you think it was?'

'I don't know.'

'Maybe it was some sort of cat.'

'Well, it would have to be a pretty big one to do that.'

'Maybe it was,' said Sandy, 'a big cat I mean.'

'Aye, maybe it was, and maybe it wasn't. I hope you aren't going to start on about all of that Beast of Rubbish, cause we don't need it here.'

'But what if there is a big cat attacking livestock?'

'One day, one of us'll get it, or it'll move on. End of story. I don't want anything in the papers. I've read about farmers made to look ridiculous, or with the army trampling all over their crops like in Cornwall, and for what? The thing, even if it exists in the first place, goes to ground.'

'Well, I'll believe that there are big cats in Scotland when one jumps out and bites me on the nose,' said Mrs. McPherson, as though that settled it.

'There are those Kellas cats, though, I think that's been proved,' said Bruce, smiling at his little brother. 'I've seen pictures of those. Gamekeepers shoot them sometimes.'

Alex saw Katrina's mouth drop open. He gave her a look that meant 'don't say anything.'

'What's a Kellas cat?' he asked.

'Bloody ugly beasts,' said Bruce. 'Sort of a wild cat. Much bigger than a moggy, skinny, with fangs and a pinhead. And they're black, not like your Scottish wild cat, which is just an overgrown stray tabby with a busy tail and temper from what I've heard.'

'How big do you think they are, these Kellas cats?' asked Sandy.

'Oh, I don't know,' said Bruce passing his plate for another helping of pie. 'Bigger than a domestic cat, or nobody would've noticed. They're meant to be fierce, but not big and bad enough to take on a heifer.'

'I never heard of a Kellas cat before,' said Alex.

'They're quite a local thing, though I think there are books about them. I saw the woman who discovered them on TV. I remember a keeper had shot one and kept it in his freezer for her.'

'Oh!' said Katrina. 'That's horrible!'

'Would you rather they were taking pheasants then?' Mr. McPherson asked her.

'If they're a rare species, then yes,' said Katrina.

'Well lassie, you might not think that if the birds were your living.' Don't say anything else, Katrina, Alex willed her.

'That's really interesting, a new species, just hidden in the Highlands,' Alex said, trying to steer things away from Katrina's anger at farmers shooting anything they didn't like.

'Maybe they're some sort of cross-breed,' said Mrs. McPherson. Alex looked at her – her sharp beak, her bright plumage – maybe she was some sort of cross-breed with a pheasant. McPherson, McPheasant. There could be a link.

Alex remembered a wildlife show he'd seen about moorland. Pheasants weren't even native to Britain, they were from somewhere like India. Rabbits weren't native either. And there were green parakeets in London. If those animals could move in and adapt, why not something else? What did a cat need, but somewhere to hunt, something to hunt, and somewhere to hide? If they could survive in the mountains in Canada or California or Spain, why not in Scotland?

'Sandy, you should talk to these two's uncle,' said Mr. McPherson. 'He's the wildlife expert.'

'We will,' said Sandy.

As they made their way to the barn where the bikes were kept, Katrina said, 'If there were these Kellas cats, that nobody said anything about, just quietly living in the wild, that could mean that other creatures could be out there without anybody being sure. Lynxes used to live in Scotland. Maybe they just never died out. Or maybe there are escaped pets, or pets that got too big and people just let them go. That website said that in 1970-something there was a new law about exotic pets and people just let them go. Maybe they survived. Maybe they bred.'

'They could mostly eat deer,' said Sandy. 'So they wouldn't be killing farm animals all the time. They could keep to the woods and forests.'

'Oh, Alex,' said Katrina, stopping dead. 'That deer! We hadn't even thought about that deer.'

'What deer?' said Sandy.

'A deer in the forest, near the Visitor Centre. It was half-eaten. But it was up a tree. Something must have pulled it there. And we were right by it. But then when Uncle Archie went back later, it had gone! Leopards do that.'

'We were right where a big cat might have been. Maybe it was watching us, stalking us even, thinking that we were going to take its prey,' said Katrina. 'I think we really should talk to Uncle Archie. There might be real danger – to people and the cat. It would be awful if somebody shot a lynx or a puma or a leopard or whatever…'

After a few circuits of the yard, the twins found they could still ride bikes. Sandy's mum called him in; he had farm chores to do. Katrina and Alex thanked her and set off, a bit wobbly at first, the dog accompanying them down the drive. They had to stop to open and then close the McPherson's huge gate. Once they were outside Alex said,

'We shouldn't really cycle. Do you remember that programme where the mountain biker in California was attacked by a puma? If you're bent over they might think you're prey.'

Katrina looked a bit pale.

'Well we've got to get home somehow. We can't ring Aunty Clara and say, please come and get us, we're frightened we might be attacked by a puma.'

Alex laughed. 'It might be true though – the heifer, the deer, the scratch marks, what I saw, the frightened dog you saw.'

'Ok. Then we'll sing. That will scare it away.'

It was hard to cycle up the hills and sing at the same time, but *Octopus's Garden* got them home.

When they got back, Clara was in the garden, looking a bit worried.

'Alex, Katrina! Nice ride? How was it at the McPherson's ?'

'It was fine. The puppies are getting really big. We had to have lunch with Mr. McPherson and one of the brothers, but that was ok. Their house is enormous, like a mansion. The heifer's getting better. But they don't know what did it. We thought, well…' said Katrina, her voice trailing off at the end.

'I talked to your mum again today. She's sounding lots better. She's coming out in a week or so.' Clara hugged them. 'It sounds like she's been doing some really serious thinking, facing up to things…she wants to do things differently in the future. It'll be really hard for her when she first comes out. I said I'd go down there, be with her at first, then she can come up and join you here.'

'But I don't know when the orchestra are back,' said Katrina. 'She'll have to see about that too. She's always saying that if she doesn't play, we don't eat.'

'Well, she'll be looking at lots of things,' said Clara. 'And I'll help her. You can help by being happy here with Archie so she knows she doesn't have to worry about you.'

'*We're* the ones who worry about *her*,' said Alex.

'Well that's one thing that's going to change,' said Clara. 'She'll get better, and Archie and I will be there to help, and we'll always be there to look after you.'

Yeah, hundreds of miles away, thought Alex. And he wandered away to swing on the tyre. The scars on the tree were looking less fresh. He expected that they'd always be there, they might fade and the bark might grow back, but he'd always know that they were there.

Chapter 16

Dusk was falling. The purple shadows were reaching out from the mountains. Alex and Katrina lay on the floor watching a documentary about volcanoes. Katrina was finding it pretty boring, but she couldn't think of anything else to do. Uncle Archie seemed to like it, and the remote was always his in the evenings. Aunty Clara was in her studio.

'Scotland's volcanic you know,' Archie told them. 'Edinburgh's built on a volcano.' Katrina imagined streams of scarlet lava flowing towards them, Inverness being engulfed, The Leisure Pool bursting into flames. They'd have to grab Mr. Tom and the hens and get a boat and row out into the centre of the loch.

Then Clara came bursting in.

'I can't find Gertie! I went to lock them up, and she's gone! She's not with the others. They've all gone in, but she's missing!'

They rushed outside and started to search. Uncle Archie went straight to the henhouse. He bent down and counted. He shook his head. Only seven.

'Don't lock the door yet,' said Clara. 'She might be nearby, laying an egg or something...'

They looked everywhere. Archie went over the wall and looked in the forest. Nothing. They searched the garden. Nothing.

'If a fox comes,' said Clara, 'it's horrible. They usually kill and injure lots and leave them, or at least leave feathers. I'm sure we'd have heard something. There'd be some sign. Oh, I hope she's not hurt or ill somewhere!' Aunty Clara's face looked pale and pinched in the gathering darkness. Archie fetched torches and they carried on searching under bushes and in the barn. Perhaps she'd got in there when they put the bikes away. She could have made her own little nest, but no. Alex lay on the gravel and looked under the cars. Nothing. They circled the garden with the torches. Nothing. There were no signs of a struggle. No little heaps of feather. Just nothing. It began to get too dark to see anything. Aunty Clara went back to the henhouse. She counted the hens again. Could Gertie have miraculously returned and slipped back in without them noticing? But no, there were still only seven there. Clara hesitated, her hand poised over the little door.

'I can't bear to lock her out. What if she comes home and she can't get in?'

'You'd better lock them in, love' said Archie. 'If there's a fox about it might be back.'

Clara nodded. She locked the door and checked all around the henhouse one last time. She shone the torch up trees incase she'd gone to roost up one. Alex fetched Mr. Tom's carrier.

'She can go in here if she comes back in the night,' he said.

'Thanks Alex,' she said, and burst into tears. Uncle Archie put his arm around her, and the twins followed up the path towards the open front door. Yellow light streamed outwards.

'I've never seen her cry before,' Katrina whispered.

'Me neither,' said Alex.

'Not like Mum,' said Katrina. They'd seen their mum cry too many times to count.

The volcano show was over and The News was on. Archie put it off. There were huge moths flapping around the lampshade. Katrina sat as far away from them as possible. Mr. Tom was on Archie's chair, watching the moths, looking kind of pleased. Clara and Archie sat down on the sofa. The twins didn't know what to do.

'Maybe she'll be back tomorrow,' said Katrina.

'Sweetheart, she's probably gone,' Clara said, scrubbing at her eyes. Mr Tom leapt from the sofa, trying to catch a moth.

'Oh Archie,' Clara said, eyeing him, 'you don't think…he couldn't have…'

'Don't be silly. He wouldn't. Domestic cats don't kill hens.'

'He wouldn't!' Alex shouted. 'He'd never hurt them!'

'He liked them!' said Katrina. 'He liked sitting and watching them…' her voice trailed off. Mr. Tom leapt again. This time he swatted a huge brown moth. It flapped horribly beneath his paw and in a moment he had it in his mouth. A wing protruded, fluttering horribly like a feather.

'Get him out of here!' Archie barked. Alex lunged, scooped up Mr. Tom and ran upstairs with him. Katrina listened to her brother's feet on the wooden stairs. His bedroom door slammed. She didn't know what to do. Should she follow Alex or stay and try to comfort Aunty Clara and defend Mr. Tom? She felt the tears welling up. She swallowed.

'I really hope Gertie's alright, Aunty Clara, and, but, I don't think it was Mr. Tom. He doesn't even catch small birds in London.' Although, she thought, there weren't that many small birds where they lived.

'He couldn't take a hen,' said Archie. 'It wouldn't happen.'

'I'm sorry,' said Clara. 'I was just being silly. It's all just so odd and not like a fox attack. and I'm so worried about Gertie, but it looks like she's gone.'

'It's just the countryside,' said Archie. 'Things get taken, preyed upon. Probably a one-off, something opportunistic, a bird of prey maybe. They'd just take one and wouldn't leave anything behind. It happens. There's nothing anyone can do.'

'I'll go and apologise to Alex and Mr. Tom,' said Clara. Katrina followed her up the stairs, but Alex was already asleep, or at least doing a very good impression of a sleeper. Mr. Tom was curled up beside him. The moth was nowhere to be seen.

Chapter 17

There was still no sign of Gertie the next morning. Alex came down after Uncle Archie had already left for work.

'I'm sorry about last night,' Aunty Clara told him. 'I know it couldn't have been Mr. Tom. I was just upset.' She still looked pretty upset.

'That's alright,' said Alex. He took the plate of toast she offered him.

'She's still not back,' said Clara. 'Archie thinks a bird of prey…. they could just swoop down and take one. There might not be any sign of a struggle. I suppose it would be swift and painless. She wouldn't know anything about it. I hope the others didn't see anything. Or if they did that they'll know to hide next time.' Katrina gave her aunty a hug. 'It happens with hens,' Clara went on. 'You have to know you might lose some. Gertie had a lovely life. I just hope the others aren't taken.'

'I wish I knew what it was,' said Alex. 'I mean, it could have been something else, something wild, like a ...' Aunty Clara looked as though she might start crying again. Katrina gave him a look. He shut up and ate his toast.

'I know,' Katrina. 'Let's make a scarecrow.' Clara smiled.

'Good idea.'

'Can we use real straw from the barn? Like in *The Wizard of Oz*? And some of Archie's old clothes?'

'All of Archie's clothes are old clothes,' said Clara, laughing but wiping tears away again.

The scarecrow did look exactly like Uncle Archie. Clara and Katrina put him up by the henhouse. Alex hadn't wanted to help. He borrowed some binoculars and spent the morning at the top of the tree with the tyre, or looking out from the hayloft or his bedroom window, endlessly scanning the area for signs of the predator. He didn't see anything. Alex was the only one inside when the phone rang. He shouted for Aunty Clara – he didn't much like answering phones – but nobody came so he picked it up himself.

'Is that young Katrina?' a voice barked at him.

'No. It's Alex.'

'This is Jean McPherson, Sandy's mother. I have a wee favour to ask your aunt.'

'I'll get her,' said Alex. He walked as slowly as he thought decent out into the garden. He supposed Mrs McPherson must want to borrow something. He hoped she wouldn't say anything mean to Aunty Clara about them, or the hens. He swung in the tyre whilst Aunty Clara went inside. The scarecrow looked quite cool. He half-wished he'd helped with it. Katrina was pretty good at making things, even though she wasn't that great at drawing. It was strange though, although he didn't want Aunty Clara to lose any more hens, he didn't really want to keep the predator away. He was pretty sure he knew what had taken Gertie, and it wasn't a fox or a bird of prey. It certainly wasn't Mr. Tom. Perhaps, rather than keeping it a bay, they should be luring it. If they could get proof, a picture or paw prints or something, people would have to believe them.

Aunty Clara came back smiling and with her arms folded, as though she was trying to look jolly. "Jolly" was one of Alex's most hated things.

'Guess what, twins?' she said. (People saying "guess what?" and people calling them "twins" were some of his other most hated things.) 'Sandy McPherson's coming for a sleepover tomorrow. The parents are off to a show and he asked if he could come to us, rather than stay with his big brother.'

'He'll have to stay in Alex's room,' Katrina said quickly. 'He's a boy.' Aunty Clara looked questioningly at Alex.

'He's ok,' said Alex. 'And they did lend us the bikes.'

'I wouldn't have thought Mr. McPherson liked shows,' said Katrina. 'I went to see *Oliver!* with the school. I think he'd hate singing and dancing. Mrs. McPherson must be making him. She is really fierce. She could make anybody do anything.'

'Agricultural show,' said Aunty Clara. 'Farm machinery, sheep, beef cattle, that kind of thing.'

'Oh,' said Katrina. She could imagine that. She could imagine him looking at the cows and seeing steaks. 'They're really into beef and steaks. They have a corridor that's just freezers full of meat.'

'Can I ring Sandy back?' said Alex. 'I want him to bring something.'

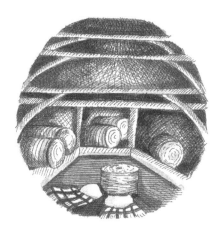

Chapter 18

'It's still frozen,' said Sandy. He drew a parcel out of his rucksack. 'Prime Aberdeen Angus. Folk'll pay a lot for these.'

'If it's frozen, it won't smell. It won't lure anything,' said Alex.

'Well the dog's would have gone crazy if I'd walked about with a rucksack dripping blood. I'd never have made it past Mum.' He smiled, and Alex suddenly felt a bit sorry for him. It must be hard having Mrs McPherson for a mum.

'We'll put it up in the hayloft. It's really warm up there and it'll be defrosted by tonight.' said Alex. 'And did you bring your phone for the camera? I haven't got one.'

'Aye,' said Sandy.

'We'll put everything ready in the hayloft,' said Alex.

'Put what in the hayloft?' Katrina asked, coming into Alex's room without knocking. She saw the boys exchange a glance, excluding her. She glared at Alex. 'Well?'

'Steak. For tonight. We're going to try and lure it. Lure it and take a picture.'

'Archie and Clara will never let us sleep up there if they know what we're planning, even if they don't believe in it,' she said. Alex noticed that she said "we", but he wouldn't really have left her out. He would have included her.

'Then we won't tell them. We'll set everything up tonight and then sneak out when they're asleep,' said Alex.

They took rugs and cushions and biscuits and string and told Aunty Clara they were making a den. Alex "borrowed" a big torch from a box of forest ranger things in Uncle Archie's study.

Out in the barn, Sandy used Katrina's knife to drill a hole through the bone in the steak. She pretended not to mind when he got blood on it, and wiped it on a tissue when he'd finished. They threaded a great long length of string through the steak.

'Fishing for a big cat,' said Sandy.

'We don't actually want to catch it,' said Alex. 'We'll let it run off with the meat once we've got a photo.'

'The flash'll frighten it. It'll make it run off,' said Katrina. 'If it even comes...'

'I don't think it'll be able to resist this,' said Sandy. The steak was defrosting fast and dripping onto the straw.

'Wrap it up again. We don't want it to come before we're here,' said Katrina. 'And all of these flies...yuk.'

That evening they did good imitation of kids who weren't up to anything. The boys played on the computer. Katrina sat outside with Clara and Archie. Her uncle and aunt weren't saying much, but Katrina had the feeling that they were keeping a look out for foxes and birds of prey. She noticed Archie (who had

142

reclaimed what he said was his favourite hat from the scarecrow) looking into the woods every few minutes. Alex, Katrina and Sandy went to bed early, hoping that Archie and Clara would too. Sandy set his phone alarm for 12.30am, but the children were all still awake when it went off. They crept down the narrow stairs, trying not to let them creak. They could hear Archie snoring.

'That would keep anything away,' whispered Sandy, nodding towards the grown-ups' bedroom. Katrina shushed him. It was too dark to give him a look. Mr. Tom was twining around her legs.

'He has to stay in. It isn't safe. He'll be a distraction,' said Alex. They tiptoed to the kitchen and gave him some crunchies. Whilst he was busy eating them, they fled. The front door's lock was stiff, and it groaned when they opened it. There was a pause in the snoring. They froze. At last the snoring started again. They crept out into the darkness.

'Get onto the grass. Avoid gravel,' hissed Alex.

'It could be here already. Stick together,' said Sandy.

'If you see it, make a big noise,' said Alex. They crept across the garden. The barn door was open, and the torch was where they'd left it, just inside. He switched it on and flashed it around the inside of the barn, trying to illuminate every patch of shadow. They propped the barn door wide open so that the creature would easily catch the scent and not be too scared to come in.

'Can big cats climb ladders?' Katrina asked. Nobody answered. Alex knew how high they could leap, but decided not to say anything.

'Ok. I think it's safe. Let's go up,' he said. He led the way with the torch and shone it around up there too, just in case. Katrina and Sandy followed him.

'Can we pull the ladder up?' asked Sandy. They tried, but it wouldn't shift. 'Ok. Let's get the bait.'

'You can do that bit, Sandy,' said Alex, as though it was a nice thing he was allowing him to do. The steak was completely defrosted. Sandy lowered it down until it hung just a foot or so above ground level. He looped the string through the binding of one of the bales.

'If anything gives that a tug, it'll be able to get its prize easily enough. We don't want it to turn nasty,' he said. 'You saw what happened to our heifer.'

'What if we fall asleep?' Katrina wondered. 'We need something to wake us up if it comes. I wish we had a bell or something to put on the other end of the string. We should have thought of that.'

'Keys, or something,' said Sandy. But none of them had any keys.

'We could sneak back in and get Uncle Archie's car keys,' said Katrina.

'Too risky,' said Alex. 'We might wake them up, and what if it comes in the meantime.'

Katrina couldn't help but think that it wouldn't just instantly arrive at the first sniff of fresh meat. Would a big cat scavenge anyway, or only eat what it killed itself?

'It could be anywhere, miles away from here,' she said, 'though it was here to take poor Gertie. But anyway, there must be something jangly in here.' Before the boys could suggest anything

144

she was back down the ladder. She slipped on the last rung and banged her leg but was determined not to make a fuss.

'Quick, Katrina – it could be coming!' said Alex. He sent the torch's beam down to where she was.

'Shine it into these boxes,' she said. 'There must be something here.'

She lifted out some huge, rusty and useless things. Underneath there was a whole load of what looked like tent pegs. Katrina grabbed a handful of these and put them in her hoodie pockets.

'Quick, Katrina! It might be coming!' said Sandy. Katrina scurried back up the ladder, secretly pleased that Sandy was bothered about her.

'Phew!' said Sandy. 'It's lucky you're a fast climber.' She emptied her pockets, and they tied a bunch of the pegs to the other end of the string. They rattled as they were lowered into position. The children spread the blankets and cushions across some of the other bales and lay down to watch and wait.

'I'm going to have the string running across my leg, then I'll feel any movement too,' said Alex.

'Put the torch off now, Alex. It might keep it away. Just be ready with it in case we hear anything,' said Katrina.

'Aye,' said Sandy. 'Our eyes'll soon be used to the dark.'

'Is your phone ready?' asked Alex.

'Aye.'

Alex switched the torch off and balanced it on the bale next to him. It was very black without it.

'There's no moon tonight,' said Sandy, 'too cloudy.'

All they could do was wait. They heard an owl calling and another answer it. They could hear the wind in the trees. A dog was barking somewhere far away.

'That sounds like Jet,' said Sandy.

'She might be barking At Something,' whispered Alex.

'Sshh,' said Katrina, louder than either of their whispers. The straw smelt dusty, but sweet. 'But we have to try really hard to keep awake.' She couldn't help yawning. 'We shouldn't have made it so comfy...'

'Sshh,' said Alex.

They lay there in the darkness. There were some strange, but very quiet rustlings coming from somewhere inside the barn.

'Probably ...only ...mice,' whispered Sandy, sounding as though he was already almost asleep. Katrina wished that she didn't know how spidery the hayloft was. It wasn't that she was scared of spiders, it was just that...

Alex kept his eyes open. It was surprising how much you could see in the dark. But then how powerful would a cat's vision be? He tried to have interesting thoughts to keep himself awake – the silhouette of the cat on the roof, the deer in the tree, the wounds on the heifer, the scratch marks, Gertie being gone, and then Mum. He couldn't help but think about her. He could hear the others breathing, soft and even. He couldn't help but drift towards sleep.

His mother was playing her viola. It was jangly music. He couldn't see her, but he knew she was there. He couldn't get up. She was playing the viola but the bow was going across his leg, backwards and forwards. It was horrible music, it didn't make any sense, and he wanted her to stop.

He was awake. It was pitch black. The string was moving. The pegs clanged.

'It's here!' he hissed. 'Wake up – it's here!' He reached for the torch. He could sense Sandy reaching for her phone.

'Now!' he hissed.

The camera flashed and flashed again. There was nothing in the torch's beam. He swung it around the barn. Nothing.

The steak was gone. Whatever had taken it was gone.

'Did you see anything?' said Alex.

'Maybe a shadow moving?' said Katrina. But she sounded hopeful rather than convinced. Alex didn't want to say that he had missed it too. 'Did you get a picture?' Sandy clicked and swiped to review the pictures.

'Nothing. I missed it. There's nothing but darkness, and maybe the floor.' He passed his phone to Katrina. There was nothing. Alex kept shining the torch around the barn, trying to spot some trace of whatever had been there.

'We should have covered the floor with chalk or flour or something to try and get prints,' he said.

'We could try another night. I suppose it might come back again…' she said.

There was a strange, eerie yelp from somewhere outside.

'What's that?' said Katrina. But she knew. It was the bark of a fox. 'We might as well go back to sleep.'

The light woke them early the next morning and they sneaked back inside.

'Don't let on. Don't tell anyone we were out here,' said Alex. It had occurred to him that Aunty Clara might not want them to be luring the chicken-killer back. 'We'll try again, or try something else.'

Sandy went home after lunch. It started to rain. Katrina and Alex spent the afternoon up in the hayloft, listening to the rain on the skylights and doing nothing, hoping that whatever it was just might happen to come back.

Chapter 19

It seemed weird, a day later, to be the ones taking Aunty Clara to the airport, and seeing her off to London whilst they stayed in Scotland. The flight left at 8am so they had to be up and out of the house really early.

'Give mum hugs from us,' said Katrina, when they got close to the departures gate. 'Oh I wish we'd got her a present or something.'

'All she needs is to know that you two are well and trying to be happy,' said Clara.

'But I still wish…could we get something there? We've got all that money from Pippa and Brian. We'll pay you back. ' Katrina stared longingly at the airport shop.

'Sure,' said Clara. 'There's time if we're quick.'

There wasn't much to choose from. Katrina fingered the "Scottish" things. Mini Nessies and little white dogs in tartan hats who played *Scotland the Brave* if you squeezed their paws. Alex looked at the magazines.

'How about chocolate?' said Uncle Archie, looking at his watch.

Katrina chose a huge slab of Dairy Milk.

'And this,' said Alex. He thrust a copy of *Classical Musician* into Clara's hands. 'Mum sometimes reads that.'

'Good idea, Alex. Perfect. Now I'd better go. And I'll be bringing her back with me in a few days,' said Clara. 'Look after them, Archie.'

'And we'll look after Archie and the hens,' said Katrina. Alex didn't say much. He hated goodbyes. Clara gave them a sad little smile and then was gone.

It started to drizzle when they left the car park. It made the journey home from the airport slower, with the roads appearing and disappearing into the mist. Archie had the day off, but he had to go into work as usual after that. Alex was quite pleased – they'd get to go with him. Archie said that they should bring a few things to do. Alex was going to take his tracker kit – he'd read all the stuff, but not used any of it. There weren't many prints to find or animals to track on a houseboat in London. Since he'd seen the cat on the roof, he'd kept looking in the garden, but there was nothing, no prints, not even Mr. Tom's, only the scratchings made by the hens and tiny marks left by other birds. And no trace of what had taken Gertie. But he might find something in the forest, and he was certainly going to look where that deer had been. There might be some real proof.

He gazed out of the window, and imagined Clara getting on the plane, it taking off, London, The Bluebell, that clinic. He was sort of looking forward to seeing his mum and sort of dreading it. Part of him felt so angry with her, part of him longed to see her. At the moment he was content to just hang about with Archie.

By the time they got back it was raining really hard.

'Best just stay indoors,' said Archie. 'You can watch TV if there's anything on.' Katrina asked to go on the computer.

'I'm going to draw Mr. Tom,' said Alex, 'using that book Clara gave me.'

But Mr. Tom was nowhere to be found.

They called and called. Alex went out into the garden. The chickens were huddled up near their house. Were they frightened or just trying to keep out of the rain? He counted. There were seven of them there. He carried on calling. He went back inside to search the house.

'He's probably gone exploring,' said Archie. 'Cats do that in a new territory.'

'I didn't even see him this morning,' said Katrina. 'I didn't really think about it because of Aunty Clara going away.'

'Me neither,' said Alex. 'He was here last night because he was looking out of the window with me after we'd gone to bed. We didn't see anything, though.'

'He'll be back. Don't worry. He's a big strong tom cat,' said Archie.

At bedtime he still wasn't back. They called some more, gazing out into the darkness.

'Cats do this,' said Archie. 'Especially toms. They wander.'

'What if he's trying to get back to London?' said Katrina.

151

'He'll not be that daft. He was happy here, settled in with you two.'

'What if it's just his instinct though?'

'He'll be back.'

'What if he knew Aunty Clara thought he killed Gertie and he's run away. Or what if a puma's got him? Or a lynx? Or a leopard? What if whatever took Gertie has taken Mr. Tom? A big cat!' said Alex. Archie smiled and raised his eyebrows.

'There might be one!' said Alex.

'I'm really worried,' said Katrina.

'Me too,' said Alex. 'We've been on the internet – there are websites all about it. Big Cats in Britain.'

'Ah,' said Archie. 'The internet, websites. You mustn't believe all of what you read on the internet. It's like the papers. You shouldn't believe everything you read in the papers.'

'Thousands of people have seen strange cats, and that's just in Scotland. There's evidence. What about that stuffed puma in the museum in Inverness?' said Katrina.

'But that doesn't mean a big cat has taken a chicken and then a big tough ginger tom,' said Archie. 'You two are worried about your mum. You've been having an odd summer, whisked away up here. Mr. Tom's just gone walkabout. He'll be -'

'In the pouring rain?' Alex broke in.

'He's probably sheltering somewhere. He'll be back.'

'What if he was defending the hens from another cat attack, or defending his new territory and it carried him off?' said Alex. Archie shook his head and smiled.

'Whatever, it's time I shut the hens in,' he said.

'Count them. Check no more have gone,' said Katrina.

'Ok,' said Archie. It was darker than usual because of the rain. Archie took the torch and his ranger's whistle from where it hung by the back door and went out into the garden.

'Why did he take his whistle? He wouldn't take his whistle unless he thought he might need it? Why would he take his whistle just to shut the hens in for the night?' said Alex. The twins stood at the door and watched their uncle.

'Mr. Tom,' they called, 'Mr. Tom! Mr. Tom! Mr. Tom!' – desolate voices in the misty Highland night. They could just make out the figure of their uncle as he lifted the side panel, bent slightly to count the hens, and then locked it and the little door at the front of the hen house. Then he walked backwards up the path, swinging the torch so that beams of light arced across the garden.

'Seven hens,' he said. 'And Mr. Tom will be back.'

'Why did you take the torch and the whistle?' Alex asked.

Archie gave a half-smile.

'I think you believe us,' Alex went on. 'When I said I saw the cat you checked around the garden, I watched you. There are scratch marks on the tree with the tyre. We'll show you tomorrow. What about that deer in the tree? That's what big cats do. What about the McPherson's heifer? What about Gertie, and the thing that frightened the dog Katrina saw?'

Archie hung up his whistle and the torch. He poured himself a wee shot of whisky.

'Hundreds of people see them every year,' said Katrina. 'Why wouldn't Alex?'

Uncle Archie settled himself in his favourite chair.

153

'You could be right,' he said. 'But that doesn't mean Mr. Tom's been eaten by a lynx or black panther.'

'Melanistic leopard,' said Alex.

Archie drained his glass.

'You aren't going to get drunk, are you?' said Katrina.

'Of course not. Most folks can have a wee drink and be fine. Would you like some hot chocolate? I'll be your aunty and your uncle tonight. Now this is what Clara would say. She'd say, first of all, have a slice of cake and some hot chocolate. Then she'd say, don't worry, Mr. Tom'll come back. He's tough and healthy and clever. Then she'd say that if some people are worrying about one thing, and they've had a hard time of it, they're quite likely to put their worries and dark imaginings onto something else. They'll see things in the shadows.'

'It isn't our imagination and worrying!' said Katrina. 'There's evidence!'

Archie knew when it wasn't worth arguing.

'Ok. Well let's do the hot chocolate and cake thing, and see how things look in the morning. Would you like to watch *Top Gear* with me? I don't know why Clara doesn't like it.'

'Can we leave some windows open, for if Mr. Tom comes back?' said Alex.

'Aye, of course we can.' Archie thought for a moment. 'How about the wee one over the porch.'

Alex and Katrina exchanged glances. So, he didn't want a big one left open. That made them feel a bit better, but also a bit worse. They went to the back door again and called and called. 'Mr. Tom! Mr Tom! Mr. Tom!'

They went up to bed. Alex put his light out straight away so that he could see out into the garden. There was no sign of Mr. Tom, or of any other cat. Later on he heard Archie calling softly – Mr. Tom! Mr. Tom! Mr. Tom! – and then he too went to bed.

Chapter 20

The light woke Alex early the next morning. He stretched his legs out, hoping to feel a warm heavy weight on the end of his bed. Nothing. He went downstairs. It was still only half past six. He opened the backdoor, hoping to find Mr. Tom waiting to be let in. Nothing. He wondered if he should let the hens out. Aunty Clara would. He remembered her saying that there was no such thing as too early in the morning for hens. Alex wished she had a cockerel too, it could be a guard. He slipped on Archie's big coat and took the whistle, and Aunty Clara's big umbrella, not that he was scared or anything. He went around the garden, softly calling Mr. Tom and looking for any signs of cats. There was nothing. Uncle Archie appeared at the back door, wearing nothing but pyjama trousers and an old green t-shirt.

'Is he not back yet?'

Alex shook his head.

'At least the rain's stopped,' said Archie. 'He'll be back. You can let those hens out now.'

'Ok,' said Alex, and he watched as the hens bundled out of their door, Dorothy with her funny foot last, as usual. Watching them made him feel sad. Aunty Clara called them "her girls". Alex bent down and stroked Dorothy. He loved the way the hens always chatted amongst themselves, just like a gang of girls waiting to go into the cinema. 'Be careful girls,' he whispered. 'Stay close to your house.' He knew that they wouldn't. If only they were like meercats, taking turns to be on sentry duty.

He stood at the back door and called Mr. Tom again and again. After a while he just stood and watched and willed Mr. Tom to come back. Uncle Archie reappeared, showered and shaved.

'Come on, then Alex. Let's make some breakfast. I have to go to work, remember? I'm sure Mr. Tom will be back.'

Uncle Archie made them porridge as usual, and he didn't say anything when they didn't eat much of it.

'Look,' he said. 'We'll leave some fresh food and water down, and a window open for when he comes back. He will be back, there's no point in worrying.'

'Ok,' said Katrina. 'But I think you should look at the marks on the tree before we go. And I think we should do something about the hens.'

'We can't do anything about the hens,' said Archie, scraping the uneaten porridge into the bin and shoving the pan into the sink. He ran the water too fast and it splashed up onto his green sweater. 'Damn. The hens have been fine for all these years. Sometimes you lose one. An opportunistic fox or a bird of prey. It happens. There's no point in worrying about it. They'll be ok.'

'Well, they will be in the *day*,' said Alex. 'Big cats mostly stalk by night. I read it on the website. And we have to watch out at dawn and dusk too.'

Archie spun around.

'Arrgh! I give up. Get your stuff for the day and then lead me to the mysterious scratch marks!'

Archie spread his sizeable fingers wide and fitted them into the marks on the tree. Then he noticed the initials and the two little clouds.

'So, did the cat carve your initials and two little clouds first of all, and then maybe it got cross about something, and did this? Come on, I've got to get to work.'

They followed him in silence to the Land Rover.

Archie switched the radio on. It was some show with the sort of music their mum hated and people laughing between the songs. It seemed to cheer him up, and by the time they reached the Visitor Centre he seemed back to his normal self. There were three cars in the car park already, hikers making early starts.

'I've got some paperwork to do first,' he said. 'You can stay in here and look at the displays and stuff, or muck about outside, but stay in shouting distance, in sight of the centre, I don't want you wandering off. I'm the only one in so we'll be here pretty much all day. You shouldn't get bored. There's plenty to do if you use your imagination, and I know you're both pretty good at that.'

'I brought that tracker kit you gave me,' said Alex.

'We're going to look for imaginary paw prints by that imaginary tree where we saw the imaginary dead deer,' said Katrina. Archie grinned at her.

'Sometimes you're too smart for me, Katrina McCloud.'

'Help yourselves to water for the plaster,' said Archie, nodding towards the little kitchen.

They started at the place where they'd eaten the ice-creams. Only a few weeks had passed since then, but it seemed a hundred years ago.

'We should stick together, and keep talking. Noise is good if we want to keep it away,' said Alex.

'Do we?' said Katrina. 'Wouldn't you like to see it?'

'I have seen it. I'd like to see it again, but you saw what it did to that heifer. If it thinks it's cornered it might attack.'

'I never heard of a cat killing a cat though,' said Katrina, thinking only of Mr. Tom. Alex said nothing. He was glad if Katrina didn't remember any of those documentaries where lions killed each other's cubs. Leopards seemed to be the worst, trying to pick off tiny tiger cubs. If only those big cats understood that they were endangered and needed to stick up for each other.

The bracken was so tall in places that it was above their heads. How easy it would be for something to hide there, in the shadows of the trees. The sunshine made gorgeous dappled patterns through the leaves; how easily a cat could be camouflaged.

'It could be anywhere,' said Alex. 'It's just like any forest or any jungle anywhere.'

'That's the tree,' said Katrina. 'It had those easy branches for climbing.'

'Go slowly,' said Alex. 'We don't want to disturb anything. Check the ground as we go, any prints, disturbed ground, fur, anything…'

They took tiny steps. The forest floor was soft and deep with pine needles that hid the sandy soil beneath. There was very little mud to be seen anywhere, and where there was mud, there were no prints. They looked up at the tree, and the fork where the deer had been. The bark looked a bit worn in places, but they couldn't see any big scratch marks. Would a cat use the tree where it took its prey as a scratching post? They didn't know.

'Let's just wander about and see if we can find anything,' said Alex.

They wandered slowly along the little paths and through the clearings around the Visitor Centre. They found a load of feathers where a wood pigeon had met its end.

'It's like being Hansel and Gretel,' said Katrina. Alex nodded. They'd both always hated that story; it was just people being cruel to each other; the stepmother, the father going along with it, the witch and then the children themselves. They'd done all about traditional tales and stories with messages at school. What was that one meant to tell you? Don't trust anyone?

They carried on looking, but it started to seem a bit pointless.

'Katrina,' Alex said. 'All these years and nobody ever really proved about big cats being here. How are we going to do it in just a couple of weeks?'

'We're just looking,' said Katrina; but when they came to a patch of tufty, soft-looking grass they lay down on it and stared up at the branches and patches of blue sky and said nothing for half an hour or so. Eventually they got up, brushed themselves down and started looking again.

They circled back to the Visitor Centre. Archie was talking to a group of tourists, showing them maps and giving them leaflets about routes. He broke off when he saw the twins approaching, grinned and waved.

The twins waited on the squishy sofa by the drinks machine until Archie had finished. The Centre sold a few things like postcards and rubbers, bars of chocolate and cartons of juice. It had seemed more interesting on other holidays when they'd been little. Some chocolate would be nice though.

'We've still got lots of that money Pippa and Brian gave us,' said Alex.

'We could buy presents for people in London,' said Katrina.

'I've got a feeling we won't be going back to London for a long time,' said Alex.

The tourists left at last, clutching their maps.

'You can have your dad back now,' one of them said, ruffling Alex's hair in a really annoying way.

Alex felt like snarling or biting, but he managed a little fake smile.

'It's a bit early,' said Archie, when the tourists had disappeared, 'but I think we should have lunch.'

'We didn't bring anything,' said Katrina. 'We forgot.'

'What kind of uncle do you think I am?' said Archie. 'Look in that rucksack over there. Then you can show me what you found this morning.'

'We didn't find anything,' said Alex.

'Nothing but some feathers from a dead pigeon,' said Katrina.

161

It was a very Uncle Archie picnic; huge slabs of bread and cheese, some apples and crisps.

'You can have some chocolate out of the machine or an ice-cream if you're still hungry.'

Katrina had a Crunchie, Alex a bag of Revels.

'I hope Mr. Tom's back,' said Katrina.

'Me too,' said Archie.

'And I hope no more hens have been taken.'

The time went quicker in the afternoon. They helped Archie paint some of the benches outside the centre with wood preserver.

They chatted as they worked.

'So,' said Archie. 'If there was a big cat around here, and I know people all over the country think they see them every year, what would you expect to find? Let's treat it like any other animal you're hoping to track.'

'Evidence. Stuff it's killed, maybe where it marks its territory with scent or scratches,' said Alex.

'Paw prints,' said Katrina.

'They call them pug marks,' said Archie.

'Pug marks,' said Katrina, smiling. It sounded cute.

'I've found plenty of prints in my time,' said Archie. 'But I've never found any cat ones – big cat or wild cat. You don't often see them even from domestic cats, do you?'

'Well, no,' said Alex. 'Not in London, but there's no mud near us. Apart from river mud, and Mr. Tom doesn't jump down there.'

'Dog prints you find in the woods all the time,' said Archie. 'I think the thing is, cats hate the wet. They don't like getting their paws muddy. They'd go along the grassy verges rather than down a muddy track or through puddles. Treat this scientifically. It's really interesting, but don't let it get you down. There's no evidence at all that Mr. Tom's been taken by a puma or anything. Wouldn't it go for the other chickens first?'

'I don't know, not if it usually comes quite late. It was night when I saw it,' said Alex.

'Hmm. But, well, look, I'm sure Mr Tom'll be back…' said Archie.

Katrina looked down at her brush. She had the treacly brown wood preserver all over the handle. It had been dripping down onto her hand and leaving spots all over the grass around the bench. How come Alex's brush looked pristine, with just the bristles darkened in a neat line? She was always the messy one when it came to things like this.

'I think I need to wash my brush, or my hands or something,' she told Uncle Archie.

'Don't worry, we're nearly done here. I think you'd be pretty easy to track though, don't you?' He paused, and winked at her. 'But, there are other types of evidence you maybe haven't thought about. Think about how a tracker uses all of his senses…'

'Or her,' said Katrina.

'Like those trackers in Africa, they can follow things for miles,' said Alex.

'Poo,' said Katrina. 'And smells.'

'Aye. Spoor is what they call it. Poo is what they mean.'

'Cats try to be neat though, and bury it,' said Alex.

'Aye, but they do scent mark as well.'

'Like tom cats who spray,' said Katrina.

'Ocelot's wee is so alkaline that if you were in prison and you had a pet ocelot, you could use its wee to dissolve metal bars and escape,' said Alex.

'Handy,' said Archie.

'Well, we could go round sniffing every tree in the forest and checking for scratch marks,' said Katrina. 'It might take a long time…'

'Other senses?' said Archie, the Uncle Archie who took parties of kids around the trails.

'Sound!' said Alex.

'You might hear it growl or roar,' said Katrina.

'One of the ways you say a cat is a big cat is if it can really roar. Lynxes aren't really big cats because they can't. Or pumas,' said Alex.

'Well, we haven't heard anything, and I don't know if anyone else has around here,' said Archie.

'But that doesn't mean that they haven't,' said Katrina. 'Sandy McPherson's dad said that people should just keep quiet about things, or they'll end up looking stupid in the papers, or having the army marching all over their crops.'

'I think that's what happened in Bodmin – you've heard of The Beast of Bodmin? "Don't Make A Fuss" is pretty much the motto for everything around here. So creatures like those Kellas cats might get shot, and other things might go unreported. When people don't like to talk about things you get mysteries and secrets and sometimes conspiracy theories, do you know what those are?' The twins nodded.

'Fake news and secret plots about alien abductions and stuff,' said Katrina.

'But although things are shadowy, there are always explanations,' said Archie. 'And I'm sure that the explanation for Mr. Tom going missing is that he is being a typical tom cat, exploring his territory. And poor old Gertie was taken by some very ordinary predator. Clara didn't really think it was Mr. Tom, she was just upset. Ok, lecture over. I think we're done here.' He stood up, stretching out his back. Katrina wiped her brush on the rag he offered her and looked down at the sticky brown marks all over her hands.

'It's going to take a fair bit of scrubbing to get those paws clean, then we'll go down to the village, get something for tea,' said Archie, smiling.

The woman in the shop knew them now, and she smiled and asked if they were enjoying their holidays. Katrina thought of The Nice One and The Nasty One in the shop at home in London. It seemed so far away; but soon Mum would be out of the clinic. They were going to see her soon. Archie bought them cheese and onion pasties for dinner.

'You'll be going back for school soon, will you?' the shop-lady said. 'Our schools are back next week.'

'Aye,' said Archie. 'We'll have to think about that won't we.' The twins nodded.

They walked along the shore, and Archie and Alex stopped to skim stones. Katrina really needed to be by herself. Her mind whirled with thoughts of Mum and school and London. She walked along by the water's edge, her hands deep in the pockets of her jeans. She went as far as she could, leaving the others far behind. Eventually she came to the boulders where the beachy bit ended and the forest began. She could see where a stream flowed beneath them, carrying water down from the mountains, through the forest and out into the loch. Katrina climbed onto the first of the boulders and then leapt nimbly from one rock to the next, trying to follow the stream back up to where it emerged from the darkness of the trees. The pebbles and shingle turned to sand at the water's edge. She saw something glinting between the stones; she bent down to see what it was. Could it be a coin, a piece of jewellery? Oh, nothing but a bit of foil, a sweet wrapper. She bent to pick it up. Beachcombers were meant to pick up litter as well as treasures. And then she saw them – some prints, a set of huge paw prints. They were about a metre apart, just close to the edge of the stream. Cat. She was sure that they had been made by a cat. She stared and stared. There was one central mark surrounded by four smaller ones, no claw marks. She closed her eyes for a moment. Had she really seen them? Were they really there? But when she opened her eyes, there they still were. Katrina looked at her own hands. She made fists. The prints were bigger than her fists. But where was the cat now? She hardly dared to look away from the marks, in case she lost them, but she looked up for a second and yelled,

'Alex! Quick! I've found something!'

They heard the urgency in her voice, and started to come towards her, still gripping the stones they were about to skim.

'Quick!' she shouted. 'There's something here!'

Alex was quick across the rocks, and was soon beside her. Uncle Archie was a little slower.

'Look!' said Katrina. 'There! Prints! I just know they're something.' She pointed and the three of them leant out over the rocks. 'There, by the stream!' Katrina looked from the prints to Alex and Archie and back again. Nobody said anything for a moment. Alex's mouth hung open. Uncle Archie looked and looked.

'Katrina,' he said, 'you didn't make them, did you, for a joke?'

'I didn't, I swear, I really didn't. I saw something glinting, and I wondered what it was, and I reached to get it, and then I saw them, there in the sand.'

Archie let out a long slow whistle. He slowly shook his head from side to side.

'These are interesting,' he said, 'very interesting.'

'What do you think they are?' Alex asked.

'Well, it's hard to be sure, but it's something big, bigger than most dogs. But there are no claw marks. That rules out lots of things – dogs, fox, badger, otter. Much too big for an otter anyway. Right shape, but too big for a wildcat.'

'I've got my tracker kit and book in the car,' said Alex.

'Smart lad. Go and fetch it. And be quick,' said Archie, glancing at the way the mountains were disappearing into the mist, if it rains, we'll lose them.' He passed Alex the keys to the Land Rover. 'I'll stay here with Katrina. I'll be watching you all the way back to the car.'

Archie's eyes flicked up towards the forest and back to the prints in the sand.

He thinks it's real. He knows it's real now, thought Alex. He won't leave Katrina by herself here in case it's lurking. And now we have proof.

Alex ran as fast as he could back along the shoreline. At one point he tripped and dropped the keys. A whole scenario flashed through his mind – the car keys lost – them all stranded by the loch – the rain starting – the prints gone. But he found them straight away and ran on.

A familiar van was parked beside Uncle Archie's. Ed Stirling, the vet, was sitting eating a Mars bar.

'Hullo, Alex, isn't it?' he said. Alex was too out of breath to answer. 'What's wrong? Is somebody hurt?'

'No,' Alex panted. 'No, we've found some prints…from a cat!'

'Oh aye,' said Ed, between mouthfuls. 'And what kind of cat would this be?'

'A big cat,' said Alex. 'I mean really, A Big Cat. Paws bigger than this.' He made fists to show the size of the prints.

Ed raised his eyebrows.

'I've got a kit, for making casts. I've got to hurry in case it rains.'

'Shall I come with you? I'd like to see these prints. They'll probably be dog or something. I've a fair knowledge of pug marks…' He glanced up at the sky. 'Looks like rain. Let's get a move on.'

As they hurried back along the shoreline Alex explained about Mr. Tom being missing, and Gertie being taken, and the shadowy cat he'd seen in the night, and the scratch marks and the deer in the tree. 'And then the McPherson's heifer. Do you think that could've been a cat?' he asked.

'Aye, it could,' said Ed. 'I wouldn't be at all surprised. Plenty of folks see them, but not many bother to report them. There have been a fair few sheep killed. One I saw a few weeks ago

168

looked very like a cat-kill. But it's hard to say. Could be a rogue dog and then foxes getting at the poor thing. It's hard to get any firm evidence.'

'But these prints…' said Alex.

'We'll take a look at them, and then I could talk to a vet at the zoo in Edinburgh, or one of my old professors for verification.'

Alex led Ed across the boulders to where Katrina and Archie were waiting.

'Look what I found!' said Katrina.

Ed Stirling let out a long slow whistle.

'Well,' he said. 'They don't look like a dog, and they're much too big for an otter, a fox or a badger…claws retracted…'

'Let's get going with that plaster,' said Archie.

'And I'll take a photo with my phone,' said Ed. He took a few pictures with Katrina's Swiss army knife beside the marks to show the scale.

'A creature might come here to drink,' said Ed. 'And this is where wee Minnie the Westie was spooked…'

Forty minutes later they were walking back along the shoreline. The twins carried a cast each.

'That way,' said Katrina, 'if Alex drops his, we'll still have mine.'

'Yeah, and if you drop yours…' said Alex.

But neither of them dropped anything. Back at the car they made the casts a little nest in Alex's sweatshirt. They were still slightly damp and liable to crumble. The rain which had been threatening all afternoon began. Ed fetched his thermos and they sat in Archie's van, sharing the hot sweet tea, watching and listening as the huge drops hit the windscreen.

'The prints'll be gone by now,' said Alex, staring mournfully out as the loch began to disappear into the mist and rain. 'But the moment we're back, I'm going to ring up Sandy and tell him.'

'We were lucky to get those casts,' said Uncle Archie.

'You're altogether a lucky man, Archie Carmichael.' said Ed, with a nod and a wink towards the picture of Clara that Archie had instead of a vanity mirror on his eye-shield 'Where is Clara? She'll be sorry to miss this.'

'She's in London. She'll be back soon with her sister, the twins' mum.'

Don't tell about mum and the drinking and everything. Don't tell him, Katrina silently urged.

'Clara's sister,' said Ed. 'And is she married?'

Archie turned round and winked at the twins.

'She's not married,' he said. 'And I'd say she was almost as pretty as my Clara.'

The twins smiled and said nothing, pretending to be studying the diagrams of paw prints in Alex's tracker book.

She can disappear. If the people come too close, if she is caught in the beams of their metal beasts, if a dog catches her scent, she will leave. She can travel all night, slipping through trees, over the heather, keeping to the secret places. There are always deer, and sweet heavy birds on the open moors. The whole world is hers.

But sometimes, when the moon is her only friend, the world is too much and she calls, she screams for a mate.

And sometimes, from far, far away, from beyond the mountains and the forest, she feels an answer.

Chapter 21

Katrina couldn't sleep. Mr Tom was still lost. Her mind kept flipping from worrying about him to the paw prints. What were they? Could they belong to a lynx, or a black panther or a puma? And where was it now? It must be out there, lurking somewhere – a big cat, wild in Scotland. And they seemed to be living right at the centre of its territory. She lay there imagining it. Had it seen them? Perhaps it had been watching them, stalking them, and would be ready to pounce at any minute. And then her mind would flip channels to start thinking about her mum. She would soon be out of the clinic and Aunty Clara was going to bring her back to Scotland. They were saying that Mum was better. But was she *really* better? Would she be better for ever, or just until another time? Was there anything that they could do? Were they meant to pretend it wasn't there, lurking, and that it might strike at any moment?

Perhaps if she put the lamp out it would be easier to get to sleep. It had been a muggy day and it was hot up in the attic. Uncle Archie had opened the windows to try and make more of a breeze. Perhaps Mr. Tom would come back in the night, he might even come in through a window. She longed for him to come back. She tried not to think of him out there, lost in the forest. What if he couldn't find anything to eat? What if the big cat got him? Hot tears soaked into her pillow. In the end she had to turn it over before she could finally fall asleep.

Something woke her, a noise in the darkness, something faint, like some creature crying far away. There was moonlight coming through the gap between her curtains. She sat up. The noise had stopped. Was Alex crying? The sound came again, but from somewhere outside. It wasn't an owl. It was higher and sadder sounding, pitiful. She listened really hard, but it stopped again and all she could hear was Uncle Archie's snoring.

She tiptoed across the landing to Alex's room.

'Alex, wake up,' she hissed. 'Wake up! There's a noise outside.' She sat down on the edge of his bed and nudged his leg, then shook it. 'Wake up Alex, there's something outside.'

He sat up, wide awake straight away, his face ghostly pale in the moonlight.

'There's a creature crying somewhere outside,' she said.

They crept down their little staircase and paused outside Uncle Archie's room. He was still snoring. Katrina shook her head and they crept on down the other flight of stairs to the front door.

Alex unlocked it, and they stood there and listened. Nothing. They stared out into the night.

'Maybe you dreamt it,' he said.

'I heard something. A crying noise, but a creature. Anyway, this is the wrong direction. It was from somewhere outside our bedrooms.'

They went to the back door and unlocked that.

'What if it's the cat, the big cat?' said Katrina.

And then Alex heard the noise, high-pitched and eerie, calling them through the darkness.

'It sounds like it's near Aunty Clara's studio,' he said. They slipped their bare feet into their trainers and stepped outside. The crying noise stopped, but a scratching, scrabbling noise started.

'It's *inside* the studio!' said Katrina. The heavy iron key would be on its hook by the door. She slipped back inside to get it. They crunched across the gravel. The scrabbling went on, becoming more frantic as they got closer.

'We're coming! We're coming!' shouted Katrina.

The lock was stiff. It took two hands to turn the key. They pushed the door open. A feline face looked up at them and meowed.

'Mr. Tom!' said Alex, kneeling down.

'Mr. Tom!' said Katrina, tears coming again. 'Oh, Alex. He's been trapped in here ever since Aunty Clara went to London!' She scooped him up. He felt thinner and lighter. 'He must be starving!' She held him tight whilst Alex locked the door again, and they turned to go back to the house. A silhouette in the light from the house stopped them. It was as big as a bear on its hind legs – Uncle Archie in his pyjamas.

Chapter 22

Clara had a black taxi waiting to take Chrissie home from the clinic.

'Oh, it's so great to see you!' Clara said, hugging her and holding her tight for a moment. 'Here are hugs from Alex and Katrina too.' Chrissie felt so thin and bony in her arms, but strong, the way willow is very strong and can be twisted and bent without breaking. 'You are going to be alright? You are ready to leave?'

'Oh, yes,' said Chrissie. 'I'm ready. I can't wait to get home and to see the twins. And my viola. I've missed them so much.'

Clara knew that her sister included the viola in that. They thanked the clinic staff, and Clara bent to take Chrissie's bag.

'No, no,' said Chrissie, snatching it away. 'I'll carry it. I'm taking responsibility now, being adult, in control, one day at a time.' They put the bag on the floor of the taxi and Chrissie gave the driver the address for The Bluebell's mooring.

'I've got flights for next Monday,' said Clara. 'I thought you would need some time to get your head together, plus the tickets would have been £150 more if we'd gone back straight away...'

'I'm so grateful for all that you've done. You've just been brilliant. I feel as though I don't even deserve to have the twins, or a sister like you.'

'We all just want you to be well and happy,' said Clara, squeezing her sister's hand. 'Oh, the twins sent these for you. I nearly ate the chocolate on the plane.' She dropped the Dairy Milk and the copy of *Classical Musician* into her sister's lap.

'Oh, thanks,' said Chrissie, her eyes filling with tears. 'I don't deserve them. I've been such a rotten mother.'

'Get well and strong for them, that's your job now,' said Clara. 'It's a disease. It's not your fault. Remember that.'

'I do need a job, I mean another job, I don't know what's happening with the orchestra, I had a row. They're somewhere in Belgium at the moment. I'd love not to have to ask for my position back...'

'Well, don't worry about that now. Open the chocolate,' said Clara. Chrissie peeled off the wrapper and slit the purple foil with her nail. She passed the bar to Clara without taking any for herself. Clara took a couple of squares and passed it back.

They were crawling along. Outside the taxi window the city continued its frenetic buzz. Chrissie thought about how it must have been carrying on like that without her, all that time she'd been locked away in the tranquil prison of the clinic. She didn't want to rejoin the hurly-burly of London. She started to flick

176

through the magazine, starting at the back, where the ads for musical instruments and courses and jobs were.

'Oh, Clara! Look at that! It would be based near you. What do you think?'

Clara looked at her sister's eyes, suddenly bright, excited and smiling again. This was the Chrissie she'd grown up with.

'It would be perfect!' she said.

The Orchestra of The Highlands and Islands.
Percussionist, Cellist and Violist required.
Full-time positions with extensive touring.
Auditions on Saturday 28th August.
Inverness Town Hall. 10am – 4pm.

Chapter 23

Katrina sprinted to answer the phone. It would probably be Mum or Aunty Clara, saying exactly when they'd be back.

'Is that Katrina?' asked a sharp voice.

'Yes,' said Katrina, a little scared.

'This is Jean McPherson, Sandy's mother. We wondered if you and your brother would like to come and see the new James Bond film in Inverness tonight. It's not really my sort of thing, but Sandy's very keen, and we thought you might like to come along too. Seems a pity to go with empty spaces...'

'Um, thank you,' said Katrina. 'I'll just check with Uncle Archie.' He said yes.

'I'll pick you up at half past six. Have your tea early. I can't abide noisy popcorn-munchers.' Mrs. McPherson rang off before Katrina could say anything else. She wasn't sure she wanted to go, though she expected that would be irrelevant to Sandy's mother.

'We don't have any choice. Mrs. McPherson is being kind to us and she doesn't want empty spaces in her car,' Katrina told Alex, but he was keener than she was.

'We can show Sandy the prints when they pick us up,' he said.

Chapter 24

It was dark and misty when they came out of the cinema.

'I love it when it's day when you go in and night when you come out,' said Katrina.

'It'll be a long dark drive back,' said Mrs. McPherson. The traffic was heavy coming out of Inverness, but she sped up as soon as they left the city, driving with all the confidence (perhaps panache, perhaps recklessness) of the Range Rover driver who knows her own roads. The fog thickened as they left The Great Glen behind and headed deeper into the Highlands. Katrina sat in the front. The boys were in the back together, laughing and talking about the film. Mrs McPherson didn't seem to expect conversation, so Katrina stared out into the darkness.

Mist is her element – darkness is her element. A shadow in shadows, she slips between trees, beneath bracken. Her black velvet is beaded with moonstones of fog. She is travelling tonight. A far away voice calls her – a mate – the promise of cubs.

Katrina found it hard to see anything to the sides, but the powerful headlamps lit their way ahead. They seemed to travel for miles without passing another car or seeing any sign of life. Soon they were at the village, driving along beside the loch, and then speeding up the road towards the Carmichael's house and McPherson's farm.

The forest is ending. She must cross a hard scar of beaten rock. She hears a rumble, a metal roar, and then she is caught, pinned in lights, trapped. She crouches to spring – too late.

It was there in front of them, dark in the beam of the lights, its outline perfect, its own headlamps beaming back silver-white at them. With its long heavy tail it was almost the width of the lane. Mrs. McPherson slammed on the brakes – too late – a terrible thud – no time to scream – the car skidded – then stopped.

Her flank – she has been hit. She's stunned – cannot move – but move she must. She drags herself up, crawls away.

'My god,' said Mrs. McPherson. 'It was a giant cat. A big cat.'

'Quick! See if it's alright!' said Alex, reaching for the door.

'No! It's a big cat. It might not be dead. Nobody gets out of the car!' Mrs McPherson extended a manicured finger towards the child-locking button – but Alex was out already and Katrina opened her door and tumbled out too.

'Get back in!' hissed Mrs. McPherson. 'It's not safe! Sandy, stay where you are!' Sandy slipped out too.

Katrina linked her arm through her brother's.

'What if it's dead?' she whispered. 'Do you think we killed it?' She didn't want to cry. They peered out into the darkness. There didn't seem to be anything up ahead.

'What if it's under the car?' whispered Alex. 'What if it went under the wheels?'

She hears their voices. Some of the small ones are seeking her. She smells no fear but her own. She sees them.

'There –' Alex cried. 'On that bank!' He pointed off to the left. 'A shadow!'

The shadow stopped moving. The eyes were green. The fur was midnight black. It looked back towards them. For a moment its eyes locked with theirs. They stood and gazed.

She gazes back. Their eyes lock. There is no threat, only the understanding of fellow creatures beneath the moon. But she knows that she must go, she must flee from the metal beast. She commands her legs – at last they obey. Down the bank she goes, there is open land ahead of her, but first a ditch. She must go on, but she cannot. The pain in her flank is too much. She must rest and wait and hope for strength to return before dawn.

'Did you see it? Did you see it look right at us?' Alex whispered. Katrina nodded and silently gripped his arm. She had seen it too.

'Get back in the car!' hissed Mrs McPherson again.

'Please,' they heard Sandy say from somewhere behind them, 'please Mum, let's just take a look in that field.' But all she did was rev the engine and flash the lights.

'Get back in!' hissed Mrs. McPherson. 'I've got to get you home. We'll see if there's anything there tomorrow.'

The three of them stared into the night for a moment more, and then slowly climbed back into the car. Mrs. McPherson tutted and shook her head.

'We're nearer your house than ours,' Sandy told the twins. 'I'll come over first thing and we'll take a look. See if your uncle can come.'

'There's to be no looking without an adult present,' said Mrs. McPherson. 'I'll drive you over myself.'

'I can just go on my bike, Mum,' said Sandy.

'We'll see.'

Chapter 25

Sandy and his mother arrived just after nine the next morning.

'I've been up since six,' said Sandy. 'She said it was rude to visit before nine. You should see the dent in the car. That proves it was there.'

'We know it was there,' said his mum, 'we all saw it.'

The fog had lifted. They set out down the lane together. It was a beautiful blue morning with the first cold twang to the air and cobwebs hung with dewdrops garlanding the banks. The Highland summer was coming to an end.

'Have you got your camera, Uncle Archie?' Alex asked.

'Aye,' said Archie, tapping one of his pockets. 'But I expect it will be long gone by now, if it survived the impact.' He was dressed in his work clothes with his whistle and his big waxed jacket. He'd got up extra early and the twins had helped him to tidy up and hoover. Their mum and Aunty Clara would be back that evening.

'I wondered about bringing a shotgun,' said Mrs. McPherson. 'I hope I was right not to bother.'

'If big cats are here,' said Alex, 'doesn't that mean they are just part of nature, and we have to accept them and live with them?'

Perhaps Sandy's mother didn't hear him. Perhaps she pretended not to, perhaps now that she'd seen it, she agreed.

They walked on in silence, scanning the lane, the verges and the fields for any sign of it.

'Look. Skid marks. This is where we hit it,' said Sandy. They stopped and looked and looked.

'That was where it went,' said Alex, pointing to where they'd seen it disappear into the darkness. They scrambled up the bank and peered over the hedge at the scrubby pasture.

'One of our fields,' said Sandy.

'There!' said Archie. 'The grass is flattened.' He pointed to a patch in a ditch just below them where the long grass was crushed. 'Perhaps it lay down there.'

'And then what?' said Katrina.

'Slunk off, I expect, after a scare like that,' said Mrs. McPherson. 'And died. Or taken off to pastures new, and hopefully not ours.'

'Alex knew about it all along,' said Archie. 'And Katrina soon afterwards. We should have been listening. You've known all summer, haven't you, twins?'

Alex and Katrina smiled and nodded. Everybody turned and looked at them. Even Mrs. McPherson looked impressed.

'I can't wait to tell everyone at school,' said Sandy. 'This is the coolest thing that has ever happened. I wish you were both staying.'

Uncle Archie put one arm around Alex and the other around Katrina.

'Folk should listen more,' he said.

Alex felt something give inside himself, something like a rusty padlock breaking open. He hugged his uncle back. They gazed across the fields and away to the forest and the mountains.

'It could be anywhere,' said Sandy. 'Anywhere out there…'

'But is it dead? Will it come back?' Katrina wondered out loud.

'I don't think we have any way of knowing,' said Archie.

'No,' said Katrina. 'We can only hope.'

Chapter 26

Alex and Katrina sat on stiff-backed wooden chairs outside the hall doors. They could just about see what was happening; but they knew they'd be able to hear every note. They kept their fingers crossed as their mum gave her music to the pianist, smiled and walked towards the centre of the stage.

It was a beautiful, magical, unearthly sound – the most perfect music they had ever heard. Their mum stood straight and strong. Her arms were tanned from the last days of a Scottish summer. She wore a black dress, borrowed from Clara. Katrina thought it was the sort of dress a princess in disguise would wear in a ballet.

The music soared. The twins couldn't see the faces of the interviewers. Their mum said that the conductor, the orchestra manager, the first violin and a few others would be there. But when the music ended, the twins heard them clapping, and saw one of them, a man, probably the first violin, go over and shake their mum's hand.

'They don't usually clap or anything at auditions,' said Katrina. 'You might get nothing but silence.'

When their mum came out, she was smiling and she hugged them.

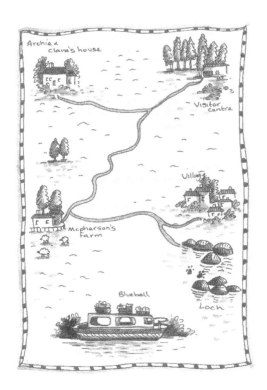

Chapter 27

Some of the Year Seven work didn't seem that different from Year Six work. There were lots more lessons, not just general things like 'topic work' but things like Chemistry and Biology and proper Art in a proper Art Room. Now they were in Geography, writing about "Where I Live":

I am lucky, Katrina wrote, *I have two homes. We have our houseboat called 'The Bluebell' which came all the way from London on a special truck and now is moored on the loch. It was amazing when the crane lowered it down into its new place. All these little kids from the village came to watch and everybody cheered when it hit the water, and then everybody suddenly broke out singing 'Yellow Submarine'. That is where we'll live when it isn't too cold and when our mum isn't away with her new orchestra. Uncle Archie and his friend Ed have made a wooden partition so Alex and I have tiny rooms of our own on the boat now. Our other home is with Aunty Clara and Uncle Archie. At the moment Alex and I have tiny bedrooms in their attic and Mum has their spare room. But builders have started making their barn into a house which will be a holiday cottage for renting out in the summer, and our house in the winter or whenever we need it, so really we are very lucky. They have a new puppy, but our cat bosses her about.*

She stopped and smiled, remembering Aunty Clara and Uncle Archie saying that they would always have a home with them when they needed it or wanted it. They would need it again soon. The Orchestra of The Highlands and Islands were going on a tour of Russia and Ukraine. Katrina and Alex would stay with Clara and Archie whilst their mum was away, apart from when she would be in St. Petersburg. They were all going to St. Petersburg. They would see the Orchestra, and meet their father. Clara had sold a whole series of paintings for more money than anyone had ever paid before, so they could all go to Russia.

So, Katrina thought, I may also sort of have a home in Russia, because soon I am going there and I will see my father, and part of me is from Russia too. She realised she was doing what her old teacher, Mr. Morgan, back in London called "digressing". But she didn't care.

I live in a beautiful place, she wrote, *I love the black-green-blue water of the loch and the soft purples and pinks and browns of the heathers. I love the shore of the loch where you can skim stones and where I found the*

191

pugmarks of a cat, a cat that might still be out there, in the darkness of the forest or the wildness of the moors and mountains…

She got up (they weren't meant to, but the Geography teacher, Mr. McGavin, was really kind). She left her place between Alys Jones (who was new as well, and didn't have the advantage of a very Scottish name or Scottish relatives) and Jessica Cameron (who did flute as well and was really friendly) and went over to look at how Alex was getting on. Katrina knew that he would have finished the writing bit by now. Alex was sitting between Sandy McPherson and Jim Ross who got the same bus as them. Katrina peered over her twin's shoulder to see the map he was drawing. There was Uncle Archie and Aunty Clara's house in the top left-hand corner, and there was the edge of the forest and the Visitor Centre in the top right, he'd shown the McPherson's farm, the twisty-turny road where Mrs. McPherson hit the cat, he'd sketched in the village, and the loch, with the boulders and stream marked, and there at the bottom, in the centre of the page, The Bluebell.

Chapter 28

November

The icy wind from the loch whistled up the hill, making the vet's eyes water. He had seen this kind of kill before, but not for a while.

- The End -

Other books for young people available from Stairwell Books

The Water Bailiff's Daughter	Yvonne Hendrie
Season of the Mammoth	Antony Wootten
The Grubby Feather Gang	Antony Wootten
Mouse Pirate	Dawn Treacher
Rosie and John's Magical Adventure	The Children of Ryedale District Primary Schools

For further information please contact rose@stairwellbooks.com

www.stairwellbooks.co.uk
@stairwellbooks